D.C. Philodemic Society

Grand Annual Celebration

Of the Philodemic society of Georgetwon college, held July 2d, 1867

D.C. Philodemic Society

Grand Annual Celebration
Of the Philodemic society of Georgetwon college, held July 2d, 1867

ISBN/EAN: 9783337223083

Printed in Europe, USA, Canada, Australia, Japan

Cover: Foto ©Andreas Hilbeck / pixelio.de

More available books at **www.hansebooks.com**

GRAND

ANNUAL CELEBRATION

OF THE

Philodemic Society

OF

GEORGETOWN COLLEGE,

Held July 2d, 1867.

BALTIMORE:
THE SUN BOOK AND JOB PRINTING ESTABLISHMENT,
Sun Iron Building.

GRAND

ANNUAL CELEBRATION

OF THE

Philodemic Society

OF

GEORGETOWN COLLEGE,

Held July 2d, 1867.

———◆———

BALTIMORE
THE SUN BOOK AND JOB PRINTING ESTABLISHMENT.
1868.

The Committee exceedingly regret that this publication has been so long delayed. Owing to unavoidable circumstances connected with Mr. Dimitry's change of residence from Brooklyn, N. Y., to New Orleans, La., they were unable to procure a copy of his oration until more than six months after its delivery.

C. S. ABELL,

W. A. HAMMOND,

D. C. LYLES.

GEORGETOWN COLLEGE, *February* 10, 1868.

CONTENTS.

GRAND ANNUAL CELEBRATION

OF THE

Philodemic Society of Georgetown College,

HELD JULY 2d, 1867.

The Philodemic Society of Georgetown College was founded
in the year 1830, by Rev. James Ryder, then Vice-President of
the College and Professor of Rhetoric.   It has for its object
"the cultivation of Eloquence, the promotion of Knowledge,
and the preservation of Liberty."   For many years its grand
annual meetings were held on the day of the College Commencement, after the regular Commencement exercises had
been concluded; but it having been found that the other re-
quirements of the day greatly interfered with its proper celebration, the meeting was transferred to January 17th, the
anniversary of the foundation of the Society.   After several
years experience of this, however, it was decided to fix the
celebration on the day preceding the annual Commencement of
the College, thus allowing to the distant members the conve-
nience of attending both the meeting and the commencement
in one visit, and yet preserving to the Society its own particu-
lar day.   This arrangement was agreed on at the meeting held
January 17th, 1867, and at the same time it was determined
to give a distinctiveness to the next celebration, by holding a
grand reunion of all the members of the Society—resident, non-
resident and honorary—and inviting thereto all the Alumni of
the College.   The President of the College, Rev. Fr. Maguire,
and the members of the Faculty, kindly and cheerfully offered

their assistance and co-operation, and a committee was appointed by the Society, who issued the following invitation:

GEORGETOWN COLLEGE, D. C., *April* 10, 1867.

DEAR SIR:

The Faculty of Georgetown College, in connection with the Philodemic Society, wishing to renew the ties of association which once bound to the College and the Society their many children now scattered throughout the land, have decided on a grand Reunion of the Philodemic Society, to be held at the College on the 2d day of July next, at 10½ o'clock A. M., on which occasion, in addition to other exercises, a Poem will be delivered by George H. Miles, Esq., of Maryland, and an Oration by Richard T. Merrick, Esq., of Washington City.

To that Reunion the Alumni of the College, and the members of the Philodemic Society, both non-resident and honorary, are cordially invited, and the Faculty hope that all the children of Alma Mater who can possibly do so, will respond to this appeal and partake of her hospitality.

To you, sir, as one of that number, this invitation is hereby personally extended, in the confident expectation of acceptance; but as, owing to time and changes, the residences of many others who ought to be present are now unknown, your assistance in the dissemination of intelligence of this Reunion is heartily solicited. Please, therefore, send the enclosed copies of this circular to such persons as you may think likely to be of the class mentioned, and also, as far as you can, by means of the newspapers in your neighborhood, or any other mode you may think feasible, communicate the invitation to those entitled to receive it, and direct public attention and favor to the celebration.

One of the features connected with this Reunion is the collection of material pertaining to the history of the Philodemic Society. To promote this end, you are requested to bring with you your *photograph*, "vignette size," endorsed with your *autograph*, and stating the date and place of your birth, your present residence and occupation, date when the photograph was taken, and, if a former student of the College, the dates of your entering and leaving the institution. It is designed to preserve these among the archives of the Society. Should it so happen that you will not be able to attend the Celebration, please send the photograph endorsed as above described, as your representative, together with a toast or sentiment, which will be read at the Celebration Festival.

As no effort on the part of the Faculty and the resident members of the Society will be spared to make this Reunion an interesting occasion, it is hoped all the children of Alma Mater will co-operate by their exertions and presence.

Very respectfully, your obedient servants,

REV. B. A. MAGUIRE, *S. J.*,
President of Georgetown College, D. C.

REV. JAMES CLARK, *S. J.*,
President of the Philodemic Society.

CHARLES W. HOFFMAN,
ARTHUR LEE,   } *Committee of Invitation.*
CHARLES S. ABELL,

This invitation was sent by mail to every one of the members of the Society and the Alumni whose addresses could be found. They extended not only throughout the United States, from Maine to California, but to Canada, the West India Islands and South America, Mexico having been excluded only from the want of mail facilities in that country. A number of gentlemen residing in various prominent localities kindly co-operated in the dissemination of the invitation to those whose residences were unknown to the committee, and the result of the united efforts for the promotion of the celebration will be found in the following pages.

A BRIEF SKETCH

OF THE

History of Georgetown College, D. C.

No one whose privilege it has ever been to visit Georgetown College will need the aid of any pen to recall the unrivalled view which is presented at that favored spot. The hill on which it stands is the last of the range inclosing the amphitheatre selected by the Father of his Country as the site of its capital, and the noble Potomac rolls immediately below. Up to this point the river is seen winding through the narrow limits of a rock-bound channel; but here it widens and encircles the beautiful Analostan, and then, swollen by the accession of the waters of the Anacosta, a mighty flood, it sweeps on to the sea. In the rear of the College the neighboring hills rise to a still greater elevation, offering to the view, first, the embowered College walk and the vine-clad ascent to the Observatory, and then, beyond, the lofty oaks which lift their tops almost to mountain height. Here we behold the solitude and romantic wildness of the dense forest, whilst but a few steps in front how changed is the scene! There lies the nation's capital, with its sister cities, teeming with the bustle of busy life; their harbors crowded with shipping, their wharves loaded with merchandize, and their streets thronged with hurried crowds, whilst from the midst of their piles of massive brick extend aloft those noble specimens of architectural skill, the public buildings, which not old Greece herself surpassed in elegance and grandeur. Beyond these, in the dim distance, the blue hills of Maryland and Virginia bound the scene. European taste has not hesitated to compare this view to the far-famed Bay of Naples, and it is at once the wonder and delight of every

2

visitor. But especially is it embalmed in the memory of those who at any time have enjoyed the privilege of a residence within the College ; and to such, particularly, it is hoped the following brief history of the institution will not prove uninteresting.

Shortly after the close of the American Revolution, the idea of establishing a college in Maryland, then the chief seat of the Catholic religion in this country, presented itself to the Rev. John Carroll, afterwards first Archbishop of Baltimore. In choosing a location for it, his good taste led him to select the eminence immediately west of the town of Georgetown, on the " Potowmac River," though of course he did not then know that the propriety of his judgment was so soon to be endorsed by the establishment of the capital of the country in its immediate vicinity. Although greatly embarrassed by want of means, and still more by the difficulty of procuring professors competent to assist in his plans, he succeeded in the year 1789 in putting up the first house, now the old central building in the south row. The schools were first opened about two years thereafter. It was first intended by Archbishop Carroll to establish his diocesan Theological Seminary in connection with the College, but this design was subsequently changed by the founding of St. Mary's College and Seminary in Baltimore city.

The first President of Georgetown College was Rev. Robert Plunkett, who assumed the position about the end of October, 1791. On the old records we find the name of *William Gaston*, of Newberne, North Carolina, afterwards the celebrated Judge Gaston, entered as the first student, on November 4th of the same year. The school rapidly grew into favor, especially among the old families of Maryland, and it would appear from the course of study adopted, that thus early great attention was given to the classic languages. It was very soon found that the first building would be wholly inadequate to the wants of the institution, and preparations were made for the erection of the spacious North Building, a great undertaking at that day. It at first progressed rapidly, but though partially fitted for occupation, owing to various embarrassments it was not finished until some years thereafter. President Plunkett was followed by Rev. Robert Molyneux, under whose gentle sway the

College continued to increase in prosperity. To him succeeded, in 1796, Rev. William V. Dubourg, afterwards Bishop of New Orleans, and finally Archbishop of Besançon, in France, and founder of "The Association for the Propagation of the Faith." Mr. Dubourg presided over the College for three years, and after him, in 1799, the chair was filled by Rev. Leonard Neale, subsequently the second Archbishop of Baltimore. Hitherto the College had been rather a preparatory school, but under the presidency of Fr. Neale, the complete college course was arranged, and students passed regularly through the belles-lettres to the class of Philosophy. This improvement took place in consequence of the College passing under the direction of the Society of Jesus, which was effected early in the year 1806, that body introducing the method and course of study peculiar to their order. Fr. Neale filled the office for seven years, until 1806, when came, for a second time, Rev. Robert Molyneux, who was succeeded, in 1808, by Rev. William Matthews, the "Father Matthews" of St. Patrick's Church, Washington city. He had formerly been a professor in the College, and it was his pleasure in after days to tell how, when the grounds of the small Mother House were surrounded by a white paling, a rider well stricken in years, but of noble and military bearing, stopped his horse at the little gate and hitched him to the fence, and Fr. Matthews had the pleasure of receiving General George Washington at Georgetown College. It seems that up to this time the presiding officer did not always reside at the College, but during Fr. Matthews' term it was fixed that there should be the President's home. It has not yet been mentioned that in early days, owing to want of room, the students did not board at the College, but found accommodations at the hotels and with families in the town. But about the year 1808 the North Building was finally completed, and that was arranged for the reception of boarders. It was built after the model of a chateau in France, and some time after its erection, the walls having been thought to be not sufficiently solid, the two towers were added, thus enhancing both its appearance and its stability. Rev. Francis Neale was the successor of Fr. Matthews, his relative and fellow student, and following him, in 1812, came Rev. John Grassi, whose presidency witnessed the capture of Washington by the British, and the destruction of the public buildings. On May 1st, in the year 1815, "Georgetown College" was chartered by the Congress of the United States, being raised to the rank of a University, and empowered to confer degrees in any of the faculties. As if invigorated by this "bill of rights," the institution increased greatly in prosperity. The successor of Fr. Grassi, in 1817, was Rev. Benedict Fenwick, afterwards Bishop of Boston. Bishop Fenwick's term was but a short one, since he gave place in 1818 to Rev. Anthony Kohlmann, who also held the post for but a brief period, having yielded in 1820 to Rev. Enoch Fenwick, brother of the bishop. Fr. Enoch continued until 1825. Then came for two years Rev. Stephen L. Dubuisson, and in 1827 Rev. William Feiner, who died in office in 1829. The next incumbent, Rev. John W. Beschter, occupied the chair for only five months.

About this time a number of American youths, who had been sent over to Italy from Georgetown, to perfect their literary culture, returned and assumed various positions under their Alma Mater, and the new life infused into the College by their energy and ability was soon visible in every department. Among them were Fathers Mulledy, Ryder, George Fenwick, Young and McSherry—names familiar to every old student of Georgetown. Rev. George Fenwick, as prefect of studies, introduced order and efficiency into the entire course of instruction, and to him is chiefly owing the present status of the "Ratio Studiorum." In this he was greatly assisted by Rev. James Ryder, who, whilst Vice President of the College, interested himself especially in promoting the study of Elocution, and to that end founded, on January 17th, 1830, the *Philodemic Society*. On the 14th of September, 1829, Rev. Thomas Mulledy, a native of Virginia, was announced as President of the College. He, with the aid of his able coadjutors, raised the institution to a point of eminence which soon won for it largely increased patronage, especially from his native state. In addition to his learning and executive ability, he was noted for his hospitality and general popularity, and by a liberal exercise of these qualities among the great men of the country who visited the capital, he gained for the College a national reputation. The increase in the number of students necessitated the enlargement of the College buildings, and in 1831 Fr. Mulledy commenced the erection of the large western wing of the south row. It was finished in 1833, and in July of that year the Commencement was held for the first time in the new Study Hall. Previously the Annual Exhibitions had taken place in the old Trinity Church of Georgetown. In connection with the new building the western half of the present Infirmary was also erected. The grounds around the College, including the famous "College Walks," were greatly improved. These walks had been first laid out about the year 1826, by Brother West, who, owning part of the land over which they extend, attached himself to the Society, and interested himself in the improvement of the ground. It was only, however, by additions and improvements made at various subsequent times, that they attained that beauty which now renders them so attractive. After a long and efficient encumbency of eight years, Fr. Mulledy was succeeded in 1837 by Rev. William McSherry, who had been the first Provincial of the Society of Jesus in Maryland. He was in delicate health during his entire presidency, and finally died whilst holding that position. The Vice President, Rev. Joseph Lopez, ex-chaplain of the Emperor Iturbide, then acted as regent for four months.

On May 1st, 1840, Rev. James Ryder was called to the predential chair. Many were the improvements introduced by that energetic officer. He instituted the periodical celebration of the landing of the Maryland pilgrims in St. Mary's county, by the Philodemic Society, and with the aid, chiefly, of Frs. Curley and Thomas Meredith Jenkins, built and established, in 1843, the Astromomical Observatory of Georgetown College. In 1845 Fr. Mulledy was chosen President for a second time, and the efficiency which distinguished his former term was continued in this. His purchase of the College Villa, a country seat for occasional recreation, afforded a delightful retreat to the wearied student. He also added, early in 1848, the eastern half to the Infirmary, and further improved that building. He was again followed, in 1848, by his predecessor and former successor, Fr. Ryder. At this period the political troubles in Europe induced a considerable emigration to America of some of the most able members of the Society of Jesus, and the faculty of Georgetown was enriched by a large accession of learning and talent. Especially in the scientific departments were the abilities of these exiles most conspicuous, and the publications of Frs. Sestini, Secchi, Curley and Ciampi evince the high degree of literary activity which then prevailed. Fr. Ryder further improved the material part of the College by the construction of the gas works and the baths, and in 1851 he established the Medical Department of Georgetown College, now in successful operation in Washington city.

Rev. Charles Henry Stonestreet succeeded Fr. Ryder in 1851, but after a term of one year he was appointed Provincial of the Society of Jesus, and gave up the chair to Rev. B. A. Maguire, then only thirty four years of age. Under his administration the prosperity of the College received even a greater impetus, and the list of students reached a higher number than had ever before been attained. The publications of Frs. Sestini and Curley showed a continuation of the literary activity. The erection, in 1854, of the large new building for juvenile students, an improvement long desired, afforded the increased accommodation the growing wants of the institution demanded. To effect this improvement it was found necessary to approach rather near the old Community burial ground lying southeast of the College, and consequently the bodies resting there were moved to the beautiful and romantic spot where they now repose. At this time, too, the green-house was built and the gardens thereto attached were laid out. In 1850 a magnificent altar of elaborately carved mahogany had been brought to the United States by Benjamin Green, Esq., United States commissioner to the island of Hayti, which had been taken from the ruined Jesuit church in the city of St. Domingo. Mr. Green had placed it at the disposal of the Archbishop of Baltimore, who presented it to Georgetown College. On its arrival there a special building was erected for its reception, and it was put together in all its old proportions, as well as space would allow. But the erection of the "small boys' building" required its removal, and it being too large ever to be placed entire in any church in this country, it was taken to pieces, and portions of it were used from time to time for the adornment of various churches. Fr. Maguire was continued in office for a term longer than is usual under the regulations of the Society, and was not followed by his successor, Rev. John Early, until the latter part of 1858. The opening of Fr. Early's administration was marked by a continuation of the prosperity attained under his predecessor, but the culmination of the political troubles of the country, in 1861, could not have failed to produce a most marked effect upon an institution situated directly midway between the contending sections, and immediately in the suburbs of a city, the "bone of contention" of the belligerents. Everything remained, indeed, remarkably quiet at the College, its patrons not seeming to heed the rising of the tempest until the bombardment of Fort Sumter, the secession of Virginia, and the call of President Lincoln for troops to suppress the rebellion. Then a sudden panic, as it were, seemed to seize the students, and every one was eager to rush to his home. In a few days the number was diminished from above three hundred to below one hundred ; and well was it so, for the troops that were pouring in for the succor of Washington city, being without accommodations, Georgetown College was seized on as a barrack. On Saturday, the 4th of May, 1861, those peaceful shades, never more beautiful than on that lovely spring evening, were occupied by the 69th, an Irish regiment, of New York militia. Nearly the whole of the main south row was filled by the soldiery, the professors and few remaining students being crowded into the north building and the upper stories of the Infirmary. The change was so sudden that although notice was given only about the usual time for dismission of evening class, the occupation was completed before dark, and the tone of military command, the tramp of the drill, and the sound of drum and fife, filled the hall which erst had re-echoed but to the voice of instruction or the hum of study.

The 69th remained at the College for several weeks, and then passed over into Virginia, on the first occupation of that State by the Federal troops. During their stay at Georgetown a scene was daily visible, which, later in the war, seemed curious enough—that of the bridges over the Potomac being guarded at either end by soldiers of the respective belligerents, and passage being freely allowed to all comers and goers. The 69th was succeeded at the College by the 79th, a Scotch regiment, of New York. These remained until the 4th of July, that day significant of freedom witnessing the liberation of the institution from military control. Notwithstanding this rude shock, old Georgetown was not in the least disturbed from her equanimity. Even when a knowledge of the watchword was necessary to enable its inmates to pass from one part of the house to another, the scholastic exercises were regularly kept up, and continued to the end of the term; and the next year opened in September with a small number of students, it is true, but with all the classes regularly organized.

In spite of the mighty war raging around her, she continued during the year to recover slowly her prosperity; but the second battle of Bull Run happening in her immediate vicinity in 1862, during vacations, she was again seized on. The same space formerly occupied as a barrack now afforded an hospital, and for another year Georgetown gave up her normal duties—this time to yield place to the wounded, the sick and the dying. At length the erection of the large hospitals around Washington relieved her, and in the latter part of 1863 she was again free. Still her list of students continued to show the effects of the war; but when peace returned, in 1865, she immediately felt its invigorating impulse, and rapidly was her number recruited. The close of President Early's career was blessed by a return of the same prosperity which marked its opening, and after a term of more than seven years, during which he conducted the College with success through a period of severe and unexampled difficulty, he retired, January 1st, 1866, to give place, for a second time, to Rev. B. A. Maguire. The term of the present incumbent has already been marked, not only by a great accession to the number of students, but by many material improvements. Chief among these are the very considerable enlargement of the play-grounds, the embellishment of the towers, and the general renovation of the College buildings. These are understood to be but the precursors of further improvements, especially the erection of a large edifice demanded for various purposes, but particularly for the better accommodation of the valuable library. It is also designed to give the Chapel the distinctiveness of a separate building. The friends of the institution may therefore congratulate themselves that not only are the difficulties induced by the war now over, but a career of even more than former success may be confidently expected for old *Georgetown College.*

Future Celebrations of the Philodemic Society.

Hereafter the Grand Annual Meeting of the Philodemic Society will take place on the day immediately preceding the Annual Commencement of Georgetown College. The Commencement for the scholastic year 1867–'68 will be held on Thursday, July 2d, 1868. Arrangements have accordingly been made for the next Celebration on Wednesday, July 1st, and all the members of the Society and the Alumni of the College are cordially invited to be present.

The Photographic Album.

In conformity with the notice contained in the invitation circular, a Photographic Album has been prepared for the reception of the photographs of the members of the Philodemic Society and the Alumni. This feature of the celebration appears to have been received with great favor, and the Album already contains the likenesses of a large number of gentlemen, and forms a most interesting collection. As it is desired to preserve the portraits of *all* the members and Alumni, together with the data specified in the circular, it is hoped that all those who have not yet done so will at an early day forward their photographs to the College.

ORATION

BY

Hon. ALEXANDER DIMITRY, of La.

OF THE

Graduating Class of 1817.

•
———————————•◆•———————————

Thirty-three years ago—the usual period allowed for the action of one generation and the incoming of its successor—I had the honor, as I now have, of standing here to speak within the walls of this Institution, so long and so faithfully consecrated to the purposes of the intellect. Since that period many a change, inseparable from all things human, has taken place. Within the peaceful precincts of this little world—the holy land of our youth—we of the elder years now look in vain for the old faces which once smiled in approval of our efforts. Equally in vain do we listen for the persuasive voices which warned and prepared us for the trials and struggles that the battle of life has not failed to bring in its course. In the outer and broader world, during that period, events have crowded upon events. Thrones have tottered and their occupants have passed away. New dynasties have sprung up, to be succeeded by other dynasties. The storm-breath of revolutions has swept over both hemispheres, and, in ruin and desolation, marked their bloody trackways. But our Republic of Letters has calmly watched the events and usefully hoarded the lessons of the age; while the Philodemic Society, gathered here in affectionate brotherhood to-day, true to the object of its institution, faithful to its noble motto, has still continued to cultivate the arts of eloquence as a muniment of popular liberty. And if, at any time, more sedulously bound to cultivate that auxiliary of influence and power, it is assuredly at this period, when the prevalence of certain moral, social and political doctrines is at work to beat down the landmarks which experience has set up for our better guidance. We hold it to be a duty, by all means, to enlarge this instrument of usefulness—this instrument of eloquence—which rescued from barbarism and led into civilization the nations of the earth when the moral darkness seemed to overspread their destinies. When the hordes of barbarians marked their way by the destruction of all that previous ages of civilization had conquered, it was the voice of eloquence which was raised to comfort the oppressed, to sustain the weak, and, with a dauntless advocacy, to plead for the cause of humanity. Especially was it so at the period when, with the crumbling of Roman power, brutal force was everywhere substituted for reason, human and divine. The days were no more when a Cicero or an Hortensius thundered from the rostrum—when consuls and tribunes, in the forum, stirred the people into watchfulness of senatorial aggressions—when the Scipios, the Fabii and the Catos had made way for the Clauds, the Neroes and the Domitians. In the midst of the appalling shock, though the voices of pagan masters of oratory were no longer heard, vindicating the right, eloquence of a higher reach, on the lips of the Basils, the Chrysostoms, the Ambroses and the Augustines, assuaged the harshness of the despotic rule, instilled a feeling of mercy into the hearts of rulers, and imposed on their power some of the salutary checks which are guaranties of the happiness of nations.

Impressed with this conviction—promised, as it were, to the defence of the people's rights, by the virtue of their device, "Eloquence, bound to Freedom," as a means of securing its perpetuity—the members of the Philodemic Society, whether those who have already contributed to the offices of life, and are here to-day to bear witness of their love to the Alma Mater, or those who are about to enter on its obligations, know that in proportion with the power of the wrong must be the power of the means to defeat its force. Well trained in the schools of sound philosophy and of impartial history, they are not unmindful of the lessons that the latter gives, nor heedless of the warnings which the former has sounded in the ears of generations, which Time has gathered in its course. Well trained in those lessons, they revert in imagination to the various regions of the globe, and revive the various scenes that have been enacted on the great theatre of civilized life. They recall to mind the continued, rebellious conflict between wrong and right, and take note of the brave effort, the baffled hope and the broken heart. They go to every point where the conflict has raged, and they find the earth furrowed by streams swollen with the tears of victims or crimsoned by the blood of martyrs; while in the very murmurs of the air they fancy the shrieks that have been wrung for centuries from the agonies of millions. They mark the lurid shadows of nations which have toppled from their places of power, and mourn over the wrecks of freedom's temples, reared but yesterday to cumber the earth with their ruins to-morrow.

Lessoned in this way—saddened, perhaps, by these scenes of desolation abroad—they feel it to be a duty to spare no exertion to ward them off from the land which has given them birth. They turn to it with a hope for the continuance of its inheritance of freedom; for the principles of a well-adjusted government; for the guaranty of laws with which the framers fenced it round, and for the opening of enlarged spheres of useful industry and rewarding pursuits. Especially would they exult in the property of mind and the blessings of knowledge, such as they have drawn here, at the fountain-heads of learning and science. But thus exulting, they cannot forget that other nations have had their marts of commerce, their workshops of industry and their altars of freedom, that have disappeared in the shadows of immemorial time. Remember these, and ask yourselves whether the future reserves any exemption for the country, unless we shall profit by the examples of the past, and prove more chary of private virtues and public rights? Ask that past to tell you the secret of the fall and ruin of states. Ask it to open its volumes, with the record of wisdom inscribed upon its thousands of pages, and there may be found admonitions, which those who govern can read with profit, where passion does not blind and injustice prevail. Nay, why should we go to other annals, when we can turn to our own, and ascertain whether we have used the best means to make ourselves faithful guardians of the legacy of freedom, of which, I trust, we may yet show ourselves to be deserving heirs? We should appeal to those annals, and learn whether we have not duties to perform as well as rights to enjoy.

This consideration commends itself to our attention under the force of peculiar claims. It is a great calamity when a generation fails in the part assigned to it in the drama of social life. Especially is it a calamity so to fail when that generation seems to have been destined for agencies which, for evil or for good, tell forever on the page of history. In such event the chain is broken, and leaves a gap in the better traditions of our race. For what is tradition but the living testimony of the past, that can no longer speak otherwise for itself? What is it but a law of our nature, long pre-existing the written law, by virtue of which, among other things, one generation borrows at its birth and conveys at its death? So that the best condition of society should be that in which a generation can borrow most of what is useful, good and pure, as it enters the social world, and return largest measures of that kind as it leaves its concerns and hopes. In this view, and it is a true one, one generation is not only responsible for itself, but it also incurs an obligation toward that which is marked as its successor!

Under this mortgage on our fidelity and our trust, what have we borrowed, and what are we preparing to lend in return? In the course of the last thirty-five years, just one-half of the term of life allotted to men, to what had been handed down to us, and which, I much fear, we have madly squandered away, we have, here and there, added many hoardings of the intellect. We have, in the prosecution of merely material developments, created more agencies and invented more appliances than all the civilized world has contrived. We have explored and worked more coal-mines than our plain ancestors had conceived to lurk in the bowels of the earth. By new uses of already acquired powers, we have seamed the surface of the country with bands of iron, wheeling over them persons and property, by processes which, exhibited to that ancestry, might have commended the inventors to the fiery rewards of the stake, or to the exorcisms of witchcraft at least. By the like uses, we have taught brute machineries to sow and reap for us, and to harvest the products of our fields. With steam to our navies, we have explored rivers and oceans which had place only in the questioned narratives of a Marco Polo or the fabulous legends of a Prester John. The sunbeam, from its worlds of light, has been impressed in our service and converted into an obedient artist, that spreads a pleasing landscape or portrays a friendly face. The lightning, which the scientific genius of the country had lured from its seat in the clouds, to guide it to the very spot where it should expend its anger, another genius now hurries over the lines which we have stretched in air to convey the records of feeling and thought, of wisdom and folly, of virtue and crime. Nay, not content with this conquest over the fields of air, we have carried the subtle agent down depths of the ocean, hitherto unexplored, and there, in mere wantonness of power, under mountains of billows, we have imprisoned it as the slave of our will, and compelled it to flash in obedience to our wants!

All these things, implying successful researches in the arcana of science, and successful applications to material improvements—all pointing to the daily triumphs of man over the rebellions of nature—we have achieved in the physical world. But is there nothing more binding on our exertions, in another order of achievements? If the injunction of the poet, "Neither a borrower nor a lender be," is a salutary one for the individual, is it as fitly applicable to the collective being called Society? We had borrowed largely of the forefathers of the land. In the political relation, we had borrowed a rich estate of freedom. What has become of it in our hands? In the social relation, we had borrowed examples of frugal habits and civic worth. Whence the luxury, the profligacies and the crimes which daily startle society? What they had not done in the intellectual circle we have striven to achieve, and, striving, we have achieved. But what marked, controlling additions have we brought to the moral world? Have we enlarged its boundaries? Have we deepened its lines or intensified its beauties? Look abroad, and make answer for yourselves; for mine might betray me into something more than the expression of a fear, that we have kept no equilibrium between intellectual advances and moral achievements. I might be tempted to whisper—that in the juncture of our political affairs the man who dares to speak openly for justice, for truth and for right, may be branded with treason; that a descending scale of morals, in our Republic, has waited upon a presumptuous standard of intellect; if it be that sounder intellect can ever exist without the purer moralities of life. Instead of the latter, judging from the spirit of recklessness which has touched the land in its length and breadth—from the disregard if not the spurning of the better teachings which foolish predecessors once held to be so many vouchers of endurance and safety to society—some might say that, far from honestly returning what was borrowed from those who have gone before us, we are in the very act of lending to our inheritors a shrunken patrimony, defaced by wild and flagitious courses, by a general impatience of restraint, by a growing contempt of right in every form, and especially by a studied perversion of the principles of a government which, for nearly a century, had made of us the object of the envy and admiration of the world at once.

I am not of those who would rashly arraign the period in which we live and move; but I regret that something less of the " earth earthy" should not be allowed to temper the unappeasable thirst that parches away every beauty from the soul, and to check the tendency of the times, which, warring against the contemplation of the higher things of life, stimulates into enormity merely material interests with their hideous progeny of lower and brutal appetites. Against these—against the profligacy—against the immorality and the irreligion which they breed—there is a conflict to be waged, that demands the concerted efforts of all who reverence the laws of God, prize the institutions of the country and value the happiness of posterity. Send forth the spirit that once stirred in the hearts of the fathers of the land; let it lead you, gentlemen, to the struggle, with equal vigor and equal trust, against the only enemies who can seriously threaten the structure of your government; and like them you may hope to conquer, and like them transmit blessings to grateful descendants. Let this be done, and we may perhaps dismiss the picture of a country lost and of institutions trampled in the dust. Let this be done, and we may smile at the generous fear that already sees the name of America inscribed on the broken column—the mournful monitor of republics overturned! But to help in averting so sad a consummation, and in avoiding the recurrence of the conflict, something else must be done. We must root out the baneful idea, which seems to have possessed us, that there is something of intrinsic efficacy in American politics, or of peculiar protection in the American character, to secure, without extraneous efforts, the continuance of popular institutions, and therefore of popular rights. For this security we must look largely to the moralizing of our youth and the preparation of their minds for all the demands of society.

Now I know no better apprenticeship of life than an education, liberal, refining and moralizing at once, such as an University like this offers to our youths—an education in which the elegancies of classical learning, the severer principles of science and the essential teachings of religion, combined into harmony, seldom fail to make of human life a sum of usefulness and worth. The mention of ancient letters, among the elements of such an education, trenches, I am aware, on what it is almost fashionable to deride. Now than these literary studies—of which some experience has been mine—I know no better processes to invigorate and enlarge the judgment of youth. They involve methods of teaching and disciplines of mind through which few of the great men of the world have not gone, and which no one who aims at a finished education can neglect, without incurring some risk of inferiority. The end and result of these methods is to excite the youthful intellect by the unceasing decomposition and recomposition of thought, wrapped up in the intricacies of languages lost to the mass of mankind. This is nothing more than the continuous application of analysis and synthesis—the two claws, if I may so call them, by which men grasp at knowledge and secure its fruits. There are some superficial people, with good intentions no doubt, who imagine that the scope of this long labor is to learn so many Greek and Latin words, soon forgotten, or at best unused. Then they exclaim: "Why all this study, when the result compensates neither the trouble nor the time, while it adds little if anything to the practical management of affairs?" Do they imagine that it added nothing to the practicalness of Jefferson, one of the most practical men, that, with a cold, philosophic eye, ever looked into the various concerns of life? Nothing to the practicalness of John Quincy Adams, the statesman and lawgiver, whom the detractors might have seen, any day, in the alcoves of the Congressional library, poring over some volume of classic lore? Nothing to the practicalness of Webster, whom I have seen leaving the glare and the dazzle of stately revelries, to borrow, in his study, a moment's refreshment from the pages of the Sallust in his hand? Nothing to the practicalness of a host of statesmen, patriots and scholars, from another portion of the Republic, of whom I must be satisfied to ask "expressive silence muse their praise?" Did the question turn upon this point only, the objection might well pass unnoticed. There is, however, another principal object, which the railers fail to perceive—the training of men who are at some day to act upon society by the lever of thought—special workmen of the intellect, for which they are admirably prepared by work on the classical languages— the object of classical studies. No, no! you must not, in your zeal to replace, as you say, "the ideal by the real," ask us to renounce a mixed system of education, which teaches the mind how to know, direct and possess itself, and accept your exclusive system of "specialties," which keeps it moving on the tread-mill of a single pursuit. You must not ask us to resign the splendors of intellectual development—letters, eloquence and the arts—for the mere wealth of industry or trade, which may be equally purchased by them. Yielding to you, we might possibly become better versed in what concerns gross perishable matter. We might probable be better advantaged by fickle fortune, which comes and goes with the revolution of a wheel. We would certainly multiply the means of securing earthly, sensual life, and, *ipso facto*, of abusing its trusts and lowering its dignity. But will we be more happy for these conquests over the dross of the earth? Shall we, therefore, be refined in the instincts of the higher nature? The answer you may consider doubtful; but what is not doubtful—what is certain—is that our civilization, gilded and jewelled as you may make it, will be less beautiful, noble and pure. It is not in human power long to preserve the moral being called Society, if it be reduced to the control of merely material interests. Its path is marked like the orbit of planets in the heavens. Like them it has laws which cannot be violated with impunity. They rest on religious faith— on the slavery of duty—on submission to the laws—on the obligations of filial piety—on the reverence of parental authority, and on the reciprocal loving-kindness—the contrast of selfishness—which convert the members of a great body into one great family. And yet all or most of these social securities the nature of your system tends gradually to dissolve. As with the builders of the mystic city, of which you have read, vain is the labor of those who attempt to build up the structures of the intellect, if

4

the labor, through human agents, be not strengthened by more than human hands. There is ample reason for this in the fact, that through the elements only of training, for which we contend, can man reach the full proportions of his nature and compass the measure of his dignity. I own, indeed, that your realistic system may bring out some of the wonderful capacities which lurk in the brain, like diamonds in the earth. Gems of surpassing lustre may be brought up from the mines of thought. Bold ideas—and heaven knows that we have ideas so bold that they have become absurd—bold ideas may flit across the disc of the intellect, like wings of eagles across the circle of the sun. The forms of mind, like the block of marble under the hand of the artist, may be fashioned into moulds of seeming beauty. But without the diviner spirit, breathing out of the elements which I have pointed out to you—a spirit giving life and power to those studies which you impiously, I had almost said enviously revile—the spirit not of purely earthly birth—which delights to ennoble our grosser nature—to bathe in the glories of an upper world—the proudest forms of the human mind, like the choicest works of the sculptor's hand, are doomed to be forever locked in lifeless symmetry. Nay, the very blaze of mere science, which too often dazzles the brain, without the beautifying influences of those studies, may, like the useless flashings of the northern lights, but serve to reveal dark and repulsive pictures, scenes of barren hopelessness and wastes of icy desolation, which no power of man can vivify! I do not pretend to the hardihood of looking into the ways and intents of Providence. Still, in the roar of all devouring cupidity—in the maelstrom of passionate greed—in the extravagance of an insatiate luxury—in the fanaticism of pretended reformers—and mainly in the vulgar ambition of political charlatans—many might trace the cause of much of the horrors which have sundered the bonds of brotherhood, convulsed the country to its foundations, appalled the sensibilities of mankind, and hunted out all feeling of ruth from the heart

And now, gentlemen, junior members of the Philodemic Society, with these considerations the duties which you are about to assume naturally connect you in my mind. If the great events which have filled the few late years have brought some distractions in your studies, they have certainly not impaired the fidelity of your pursuits. May you, at least, never forget the lesson which they have added to those of science and of love; and let this premature experience of the deadliness of fanatical madness and rival ambitions, which has gloomed the dawn of your youth, be not lost to the wisdom of your maturer years. The nature of such trials, gentlemen, is quickly to initiate men into an appreciation of the higher virtues, and, even now, you no doubt fully understand how excesses may prove less fatal, if the sense of order and of right have survived them, in the productions of the mind. The greater, therefore, the amount of freedom that may be vouchsafed to you, the more binding on you to strengthen the moral check in the heart—the more important to fortify the authority of the laws over society. But, gentlemen, the discipline which has been the essence of your education and the first condition of your collegiate success—what is it but the early apprenticeship of respect for law and observance of right? Continue, therefore, ever to revere, in the sanctuary of your conscience, the moral law, of which the written law, to be binding, must be a faithful transcript, and to cherish it as a guide of all your actions in life. In recalling, whether in pride or in sorrow, the liberties once asserted by your fathers, you will not forget at what price they were secured. You will not forget that everything that is great, good or beautiful must be purchased by sacrifice. Justice, freedom and truth are great appanages of our species; but Providence has willed that man should conquer them, like the daily bread. Attempts at their re-conquest at the price of blood have been made, and the political order of the country has acquired the sad privilege of honoring martyrs on both sides. But my words would not turn your attention to a gloomy picture. They would rather invite your minds to more consoling thoughts, and ask you, until the wounds of the country are healed, piously to cherish the memory of the better days, when there were no wounds to be healed. In the presence of less darksome hopes for the country, what can your friends ask of you, unless that you shall résolve, and, having resolved, that you shall strive to take your place among the foremost of her children, helping to soothe the asperities of the past, and to repair the reciprocal errors and wrongs of your sires?

It were vain to attempt to conceal from you that in arduous, if not perilous times, you are about to step into active life, on pathways which the unfathomable designs of God still cover with a mysterious darkness, which no human eye can pierce. No one may forecast the duration or foresee the incidents of the peace-conflict in which you may soon be involved. Before its decision, perchance, most of the generation of your seniors may have gone to their accountabilities before a tribunal that knows no error and admits no appeal, and you be summoned to take their place, with your responsibilities for weal or for woe. You have here learned the sound maxim which teaches that *corruptio optimi pessima;* and you will not consent to that worst form of corruption which corrupts the purest of things. I have no fears, gentlemen; but have every trust in you. I attest your elder compeers, gathered from various points of the country—I attest two full generations of upright and patriotic citizens, who learned the bondage of duty here. I attest you, whose present is a bond for the future. You, in this respect, can never, whether in word or deed, incur the rebuke of this wisdom of antiquity. It has been your blessing, one in which we, your seniors, once shared, to have for teachers men of high reaches of intellect, of great wealth of virtue, who, with the precept, have not spared the example—men for whom you and ourselves claim, in the words of the great Florentine, the right lovingly to proclaim our gratitude:

> ———"Fast in my mind
> Is fixed, and closely folded in my heart,
> Your dear and good, paternal face, what years
> It looked on me, and hour by hour, ye taught
> The way for man to reach eternity—
> And how I prized the lesson, well beseems
> That long as life endures, my tongue should speak."

Thanks, then, to the lights, thanks to the zeal, early and late, at once watchful and fatherly, of the wise heads and large experience that beaconed you along. You have not only fully and honorably sustained the dignity of our society, but you have also, in your bearing, given bright promise that you will not fail to supply your country with good men and enlightened citizens—given promise that it shall not want, in you, what it has too often missed in its sorest needs, and what, above all things, it now sorely wants, incorruptible souls and unswerving wills—whenever, through the voice of duty, it may call on your service, heart and brain, tongue and hand, to resist every scheme of oppression, fight every advance of tyranny, and maintain the right from whatever quarter assailed.

Even now, gentlemen, before your eager eyes, the visions of distinction and fame come trooping through the ivory gate. Yet, the noble ends to which they marshal you, you need not expect to attain without labor and perseverance, which, with virtue, are the only conditions of fruitful success,—labor and perseverance, I say, which multiply the powers of the mind and give impetus to its best efforts.

Be but steadfast to your good traditions and you will enlarge your talents. Be convinced that of all earthly goods talent, after all, is the most desirable; as it is the most durable; of all means of adding to your usefulness and your welfare, it is the most certain; of all paths which lead to place and renown, it is the safest and the most direct. It is not only defiant of the vicissitudes of time, but it also compensates for the injustice or violence of man should they assail. A man of the most emi-

nent merit may be despoiled of the gifts of fortune, repelled from the
higher offices of society, or even sent on the ways of exile from a shat-
tered hearth. But nothing can ever impress—no court ever decree away
—his stock of knowledge, which gives consciousness of superiority; and
none can ever wrest from his grasp the wand of learning, harvested
through seasons of assiduous toil. As from the spring of Marah, which
mocked the lips of Israel in its wanderings, the waters of life may rise in
bitterness along his pilgrimage; but, like the rod of the Leader, it is but
casting in the wand of knowledge, and the waters will again bubble in
sweetness and refreshment.

Do not, therefore, ask me why this labor and perseverance are thus enjoined. Do not tell me, as, in my humble ministry of education, I have
heard many say, "Is not life life? Are not comfort, contentment and
ease its crowning developments?" The crowning developments of life,
young gentlemen? The grave—the end of the true man's labors—
that is the crowning development of this life for another life! Mere contentment and ease, gentlemen, are the sure precursors of the suspension,
if not the wane, of the energies of life. As surely as the blood, struggling in slackened courses through the veins, tokens the gradual approaches of dissolution, so surely will the influences of contentment and
ease bring on the apathy, which is death to all noble or useful efforts!
Shake them off, gentlemen, if they mean anything but the ease that comes
out of useful exertions—the content which attends the serenity of a rewarding conscience. Listen not to the Syren song of ease—taste not
of the Circean cup of contentment—if the one means the song that lulled
the mariner of old into sensual dreaminess, the other the cup that washed
away the image of God from its sanctuary!

And now, gentlemen, to-morrow you pass from the silence of the study-
room and the sports of your play grounds to the calls and turmoils of the
world, with the character and obligations of citizens of the republic. As
in the days of olden Rome, when in the darker solemnities of her *Ver
Sacrum* she drove her sons, in the spring-tide of their youth, across her
frontiers to dare the chances of life, so your Alma Mater—but with a different spirit, the loving spirit that cheered and sustained you along the
paths of learning—will to-morrow hand you across her threshold to the
avenues which the future may open to your lawful ambition, controlled
by honest intents and directed by cultivated powers. But unlike Pagan
Rome, sending forth her progeny with a veil before their eyes—a fearful
augury of error—to wander gropingly through every phase of darkness,
your provident mother has opened yours to all the opulence of the beau-

tiful and all the obligations of the true, so that your young lives may not stumble in their course; so that, adorned with every splendor of virtue and weaponed with every appliance of knowledge, they may, to the last, be consecrated to the worship and the defense of the Truth, the lessons of which you have learned within these hallowed walls. Gather, thenceforth, around the Truth! Truth, from the sunbeam that straggles from a world of light to the veriest particle of dust which you brush from your path! Truth in the intellectual world, the social world, and the religious world! Truth, everywhere, at every point of the circumference of the earth! And beyond, and further still, beyond the flaming bounds of the universe, up to the footstool of the Almighty, whence it gushes from fountains of perennial freshness and undying power!

PEACE.

1.

Boom! boom! Toll! toll!
Hark, how the echoes gather and roll,
Gather and roll thro' the land afar,
    Unto its uttermost verge,
    Gather and roll with a mighty surge,
        Far, far,
Under the sun and under the star,
      With a clash and clangor
        Of bells, and a roar
        Of guns, that in anger
        Are roaring no more.
From fleet and fortress, from tower and steeple
    Crashes a stormy voice,
Till the winds sing and the waves sing
    To all the land, "Rejoice!"
And clear thro' the clamor of bells and guns,
A joyous, tremulous whisper runs,
    By meadow and mart,
    From lip to lip and from heart to heart,
From lips that quiver, from hearts that spill
    Over the eyelids their brimming tears,
Shaken in hope's first thrill—
    A whisper that wavers and doubts and fears,
    Yet wins its way into willing ears,
Till it swells to an anthem, solemn and grand,
Sweeping the length and the breadth of the Land—
    The hymn of a rescued People!
A voice of triumph that whoso hears
Shall catch his breath with a mighty thrill,
And lips that quiver, and eyes that fill
    With the April rain of a sudden joy:
    The voice of a People uplifted in praise
For vanquished terrors and past annoy,
    And troubles of darker days:
The pæan of Paul let free of prison;
Lazarus' hymn from the dead rerisen;
    Miriam's song by the Red Sea shore:
A voice that shall march thro' the listening years
    Evermore:

A voice that shall scatter the starless night
Of crownèd Wrong and caitiff Might,
    And shall nerve the heart of an unborn Time
    To lofty thought and to deed sublime
In the endless battle of Right.
    So the chorus rises and swells,
    With boom of cannon and clangor of bells,.
And thunder of voices on street and strand,
Over the length and the breadth of the land,
    Till far away from across the seas,
    Borne on the lips of the courier breeze,
      A kindred nation
    Sends faint echo of exultation
To join in the jubilant chorus of Peace!

2.

    Peace, and a land at rest
      From the toil and the travail of years,
      From the terror for all she loved best,
      From the wo that was worse than her fears :
From the ploughing of hate and the planting of wrath,
      And the harvest of blood and tears.
    Peace!   Did it drop from a star?
      Was it blown in the breath of the wind
From a happier heaven afar,
That it lay in our thorny path,
      A flower to be trodden behind
    By the fierce red heel of our War,
      Scarce seeing it, reckless to see,
    Scarce knowing it, seeing it fair,
      To be sprung of his loins and to be
Of his toils and his triumphs the heir?
      But be sure, whencesoever it came,
It came from the God of Peace :
      He hath written His mandate in flame,
        On the walls of the day and the night,
That the strife and the anguish shall cease :
      He hath broken away the cloud
        That hid from our eyes the light,
      That folded our land as a shroud,
        And lay on the world for a blight ;
And the sun and the stars proclaim
      With a mighty voice and loud,
That the wo and the wrath and the shame
      Are banished forever and aye—
He hath set up His rainbow on high,
      He hath rent the cloud curtain away,
And the face of the earth and the face of the sky,
      In the light of His presence are gay.

3.

Peace and the smile of God,
    Dawn after darkest night,
Fountain, at stroke of the Prophet's rod
    Making the wilderness bright,
Track, from the dark and the desert untrod
    Into a Land of Light!
Beautiful Promised Land,
    Longed for with burning desire,
With hope that was built on the sand,
    And fear that was fuel to fire—
Sought for and fought for with heart and with hand,
    In fury of blind desire,
With wrathful heart and woful hand,
    And striving that knew not to tire;
Till at last from the thorny places,
    From the wrath and the shame and the wo,
We found the hidden traces,
    And followed to Jordan's flow,
And stood on Pisgah's summit,
    And with laughter and tears saw from it
    All Canaan bloom below!
But our Prophet was taken from us,
    Who had marshalled the ways we trod,
To a land of yet Fairer Promise,
    To the Peace of the Plains of God.

4.

Peace! Do we realize it even yet?
    We others that have held aloof
Thro' these long years of agony and doubt,
That slowly, slowly forged our future out,
    With many a shock of battle, toil and sweat,
And blood of all our bravest and our best,
    Who risked the final test
Of virtue in the front of danger set,
    And gave divinest proof
Of love for this dear land so sore beset.
    Not satisfied to give
Mere mockery of aid, tame, timorous prate
Of "ifs" and "buts," vain hope and vain regret:
    Not satisfied to live,
If, dying, they might better serve the state:
They saw to dare was greater than to think,
    Flung all their prodigal hearts into the strife,
And carved their love on battle's perilous brink,
    In fiery sentences, each word a life.
Perchance we loved and served our country too;
But how know we what Peace is, knowing not War?

We heard the thunder from afar,
Missed from our midst some usual face and knew
God's bolt had found its mark. Our small griefs grew
To veil a day in gloom, then waned and fled,
As in the living we forgot the dead—
       And so we fought our War.
Or, if the lightning smote some dearer head,
  So bound to us by every tenderest tie
Of love and kinship that our heartstrings bled,
    And withered in us, and each household Lar
      Of Use and Wont shrieked shrill in agony ;
    And life was shrivelled in the awful blaze
    That lit to death our dear ones, and the days
    Were turned to ashes and all joy was grief,
    And hope a mockery, and a lie belief—
What in the shadow of such sovereign wo
    Were War or Peace to us but phantasms dim,
    Scarce unlike phases of a hideous dream
We see and know not, caring not to know ?

5.

Is Peace then ours? The sky is not more blue,
  The sun more bright, the summer fields more fair
With myriad blooms of every changeful hue,
      Nor sleeps in stiller swoon,
  Meshed in a net of light, the languorous air,
Unvexed by any song of bird or bee,
  Cradled to slumber in the lap of noon ;
  Not any whit more beautiful, our June
Blushes amid her roses, 'neath this free,
    Clear Northern heaven we love so, than of yore,
    When every Northward-straining breeze upbore
To us first awestruck, anxious next, and then
Incurious, clash of arms and shock of men,
    And fitful clang of battle, heard no more
      Than Ocean's faint-heard roar
In the dull monotone of its murmuring shell;
  When on the far horizon loomed a rack
  Of beetling storm, thro' all its sullen black
Seamed with the frequent lightning :—yet there fell
No blight upon our harvests ; in our marts
  Men bought and bartered, chaffering o'er their gains,
Nor recked what grim exchange of gallant hearts
  Death dealt in on those far-off storm-swept plains.
As gamesters play with cards, played they with war,
      And staked their hoarded dross
Upon the turn of a battle,—lost or won
  They cared not, only for their gain or loss.

A storm was in the land. What then? Afar
   From us it held: serenely as before,
Flowed on our lives, lit by as fair a sun,
   And all the world than we seemed shaken more
   By that wild ruin on our Southern shore.

6.

Not so, not so! Ourselves ourselves do wrong,
   That say it! Though the sordid few,
Unblest thenceforth by any breath of song,
   To Mammon gave the altar that was due
      To country,—let their paltry pelf
Outweigh a Nation in the scales of self,
And Freedom's sword were well content to yield,
But clamored bravely for her golden shield—
They were but few—alas, that they were any!
   A poor and pitiful few
      That leavened not the many:
The great heart of the People throbbed as ever true.
   Nor less than they whose blood on many a field
      Their pure devotion sealed
   Loved we this land of ours,
   And throned her queen of all our vassal powers,
   And served with incense of our brightest hours;
      But ah! less blest than they,
Round whom her proudest smile hath poured eternal day!

7.

   To dare, to dare, to dare!
      To fill the yawning gap
         Astride a stricken cause,
   With spirit bold to bear
      Any whatever hap,
         And hand that will not pause
Or stay from smiting, till the foe
Fly or fall beneath its blow,
And stubborn foot that gives not back
Only a step from its foremost track—
      Ah! to stand
   So, in gaze of all the land,
   One defiant, godlike form,
   Breasting well the fiery storm,
      Fiercely fair,
   With flaming eyes and floating hair,
   Superb on battle's windy height,
      And bright
   With battle's aureole of sanguine light:

<pre>
              So to stand,
       Poised in sight of all the land—
       That were noble, glorious, grand !
              So to fall,
       Having well but vainly striven,
       Feet to foe and face to heaven,
       Nobler, grander yet—sublime
       Death that overmasters Time !
                   His country's love shall be his pall
              That falls so, and his country's tears
       Shall keep his name in bloom thro' unforgetful years.
</pre>

8

<pre>
So your country's love ye won, high hearted,
       When not vainly rang her clarion call :
Yours her bitterest tears are, brave departed,
       Never prized as in your glorious fall.
Chosen of her sons shall ye be cherished
       Whom unscathed she welcomes from the strife :
Chide her not if to her dear ones perished,
       Tears she gives—alas ! she cannot, life.
They, when first her bugles blew the rally,
       Sprang with you to battle by her side :
Now they sleep in many a Southern valley,
       You return to say how well they died.
Yours are all she hath of wealth or station,
       Every guerdon that befits the brave :
Theirs the solemn thanks of lamentation,
       And the tear-sown daisies of the grave.
But for all her sons her heart hath places,
       Most in mourning them she praiseth ye :
Tis her joy at sight of your dear faces,
       Feeds her grief for them she may not see.
Side by side ye wrote the brightest pages
       Of her history in words of flame,
And together to remotest ages,
       Far she flings the radiance of your fame.
So they are not dead who went before ye
       To receive their heritage of light,
One same immortality of Glory
       Plucks ye both from Fate, and Time, and envious Night.
</pre>

9

<pre>
              To them be praise,
       Honor and thanks of all men through all days,
Who took their lives in their hands and went,
              At the first call of duty,
       Gaily as bridegrooms in their youthful beauty,
Thro' fire and flood and fell, strange ways of strife,
</pre>

Yet swerved not, nor were bent
Only an instant from their stern intent
To snatch a wounded cause
Out of the snarling cannon's jaws,
And breathe into its swoon their own fresh life,
Whose eyes have looked in Death's eyes—darkly grand
Imperious, lurid, basilisk eyes—nor quailed ;
Who in love's very wantonness have scaled
The slippery cliffs of doom,
And plucked from Glory's eyrie some wild plume
To deck thy beauteous brows, beloved Land !
Ah, yes, to them be praise,
Honor and thanks of all men through all days,
Fair lives and fortunes bland :
These to the living—to the dead, twice blest,
Twin crowns of Earth and Heaven, and God's eternal rest.

10

But were there not of us, too, those
Who loved and served and shared their country's woes?
Make answer ye,
To whom not any praise shall be,
Honor, or thanks like theirs, but only God,
That readeth hearts, shall see
How humbly ye have kissed His chastening rod
· And hugged your agony.
The bugle's blare
Shrilled wildly thro' the shuddering air,
And lo!
Your loved ones were not with you, but their feet
Were set on that dark track,
Where martial steps clank forth but printless feet flit back.
They went—you let them go,
And sate you down to wrestle with your sorrow,
And fight with shadows, wan, weird brood
Of memories sadly sweet,
And bitter sad forebodings ne'er subdued.
Ah me! the darkened homes
Where never sunlight comes
But always Night that knows not any morrow.
Was it the long procession sad and slow,
Mournful with flags, dull throb of muffled drums,
And wailing music, brought us home our wo?
Or was it dropped from Rumor's casual mouth,
That, somewhere in the far and fatal South,
A fair young head was low,
A brave young heart was still, its life blood poured
To slake the ravening drouth
Of those black fields ploughed only by the sword?

What matters how it came, that baleful breath,
Blown backward from the poisonous lips of Death
  To palsy Life, the liar,
That told us Death was not. Oh, word of doom !
That made the laughing Hours grim sextons of the tomb,
 And the wild Present one fierce point of fire
  Disparting twin eternities of gloom :
   A pinnacle of pain,
 Upheaved as by an earthquake's ire,
Lone in the shoreless dark of Sorrow's moaning main !

11

 O, Sorrow, sombre visitant,
  Unbidden and unwelcome guest,
 Death's pale forerunner, sycophant
  And heir of Death : whose worst bequest
  Is madness or a life's unrest ;
   Whose best,
The sullen opiate that dulls thy blows ;
  Who scatterest fire and balm,
 And sett'st reluctant chrism on bleeding brows
Thy crown of thorns hath prest ;
  Who ravest and art calm ;
Whose right hand bears the sword, whose left the palm ;
  Inconstant, variable thou,
  Annoyer erst, consoler now—
 In all thy moods the loftier soul,
 Self-centred, self-possessed,
  Drinking distraction
Deep from the mantling cup of action,
 Knows how to tame thee to its stern control,
 And bind with gyves of great deeds, and so wrest
The mastery from thee, and make thee its slave.
  But to the home-caged heart,
Whose love is all its might, its only art,
 Numbed by the viper Doubt it could not warm,
  And shrouded in suspense
 That scarce anticipates the grave,
 Thy hand is heavy and fraught with deadly harm,
  Thou comest malignant and intense,
 A very tyrant then from whom
 The sole, sad freedom is the tomb.

12

 Such Sorrow was with them
Who gave the lives that more they loved than life,
 To dim the sacrificial knife,
  To pour,
In battle's vintage crushed, the wine—
  Bitter as brine,

But potent to restore,—
That nations drinking have found health once more.
O, sacred grief! not mine, not mine,
With sacrilegious hand thy veil to raise,
But reverently I kiss thy garment's hem,
And reverently I twine
Around thy crown of thorns their blood-stained bays—
A deathless diadem!

13.

Then say not we held us aloof
Who drew no battle brand:
We have woven the warp, if they the woof,
In this mantle of Peace for our land.
To every man is given
His part in the plans of Heaven,
And, so that the service be thorough,
The way shall not be scanned,
Whether he follow the furrow,
Or in the trenches stand,
Whether he plot with the tireless brain,
Or strive with the mightful hand.
The truth that the cannon thunder.
Is whispered as clear in the lyre;
The flame shines brightest, but under
The flame is the heart of the fire.

14.

Peace, peace! Ah yes, we know our peace is won:
There is a secret gladness in the air,
A glory in the sun,
A freshness in the world that was not there.
Round us, reflected in all eyes,
We read the beauty of serener skies,
Where calm and large and fair,
Once more the planet of our fate doth rise
Past clouds of wan despair.
Peace brims our hearts: from round about us all
Our troubles seem to fall
Like cast-off garments we have ceased to wear.
With all its myriad voices
The happy land rejoices,
And every voice is loud in praise and prayer.
Yea, even they,
Whom grief holds utterly, not for a day,
But in all time forever, make them gay,
And light sad eyes with transient lights of joy,
That this first taste of bliss be bliss without alloy.

15.

Yet now the flush is over, let us think :
Is Peace mere rest, and shall we feast and drink,
Laugh and make merry, fling all care away,
And live once more our idle holiday ?
Alas ! 'twas so we tottered on the brink
    Of ruin—so came near to sink
A fallen star, forever not to rise.
Gird up thy loins, O Land ; before thee lies
    Still many a hissing Wrong,
That thou shalt set thy heel on till it dies.
    Thou suffered'st and wast strong,
Be strong in thy release. Now comes the real,
    The terrible ordèal.
Not in the press of arms, the fiery shock
Of wars that beat upon thee as a rock,
Against whose stubborn front the tireless sea
    Rears its embattled billows, backward flung,
      Forever and forever reared again :—
      Not then, not then,
    When victory in the balance hung
And trembled, trembled I for thee,
    My country. For I knew too well
How at the stern, set beauty of thy face,
    And terror of thy beautiful, blazing eye,
      Lit with the light of battle, and close, pale lips
Imprisoning Pity, foes shrank back apace,
    And, losing heart, lost half the fight ere fell
      Thy vengeful arm, with ruin and eclipse,
    On all that ever faced thy battle cry.
O, not in danger's midst is danger most,
    Most need of ready hand, true heart, quick eye.
Full many a bark has 'scaped the iron coast
    Of wreck-fed Labrador, and the white fierce jaws
    Of ravenous breakers, clamoring with no pause
From clamor and thirst for blood—hath shunned all these
To perish in treacherous calm of tropic seas
    That smile a strumpet smile, and lure and lull
With poisonous kisses into fatal ease,
      Even as the Syren's tuneful lips
Were deadlier than the shining Cyclades.
    Death hath his quiver full
      Of shafts that such sweet, subtle venom tips,
    It slays us and we know not that we die.
      O, Land, beware!
Gird up thy loins anew. There comes a cry
  From out waste places ; all the troubled air
  Is filled with prophet voices crying, "Beware !
Keep watch and ward, lest Death, the Ever-nigh,
Smite through thy dreamful leisure, and thou die."

16.

The sordid lust
Of place and power, the cankering rust
   That tarnished Honor's steel within the sheath;
The serpent greed that grovelled in the dust,
    And spawned in its own slime and fed on death;
     The blind idolatry that made
Its god of Self and worshipped unafraid:
   The social treason murdering trust;
     The civic wreath
Scorned in the struggle base for civic spoils;
   The aimless apathy we miscalled life,
    Vacant of all high purpose, only rife
    With petty bickering and fraternal strife;
These were the sins that wound us in their toils,
And dragged down Heaven in judgment; Heaven is just.
     We sinned, we suffered, we repent,
    And praise our God that made His hand so light.
    Can we keep faith with Him? hold fast to right
     And sin no more? The grand experiment
Is worth grand effort; else blind Fortune foils
   Our grasp at happiness, our toil is vain,
Peace but the idle vapor of a night,
    A figment of the brain,
And War a Sisyphus-labor that recoils
    Forever in headlong ruin of futile pain.

17.

These are our brothers that we loved of yore:
   Shall Hate usurp for aye Love's vacant throne?
They sinned but suffered too—yea, suffered more
   Perchance than we: Wrath claimed them for his own.
     Lo! where he reigns
O'er a broad realm of sterile plains
And blackened roof-trees—skeletons gaunt and bare
   Of dead dear homes—their hearths made desolate
With hollow-eyed Want and stony-lipped Despair,
   Sitting where Peace and Plenty erewhile sate.
   Ah! yes, they suffered: only God can tell
   How much they suffered and how well.
     They are our kith and kin,
    And though they earned the wage of sin
In most ungrudging measure of Death,
   They drained it without murmur, as became
   Kinsmen and coheirs of our fathers' fame.
    A frowning face
Fate set towards them and blew a bitter breath,
Yet could not bend them, an unbending race,
That welcomed Death, so Death outstripped disgrace.

Violent and rash and resolute in wrong,
But noble, but our brothers, nowise base;
Even in error they won us, seeing them strong
And terrible of hand against us raised
In battle, to praise them : spite ourselves we praised.
And justly ; for one Mother bore us, one
That wept to see us sundered, and shall write
Their brave deeds on her heart in lines as white
As love may make them in default of right.
Their vices are their own,
Ephemeral, carrion for the vulture Hours;
Their virtues are their country's—hers and ours—
The priceless and immortal heritage
Wherewith she dowers
A future and, so dowered, a better age.
Thus, then, it stands :
Shall we again strike clasp of brotherly hands,
And set our faces toward a Future vast—
The dim Sangrail of all our errant Past?
Or shall we hold apart,
Hate smouldering still in every sullen heart
For frantic Chance to fan into a fire
Shall wrap the martyred land in fiercer blaze—
Cain's sacrifice—till on her funeral pyre
Freedom shall perish with our perished days?

18.

Answer, my countrymen ! A million fates
Hang on your answer, and sad Freedom waits,
Panting and pale, her sword
Scarce sheathed from battle, to hear the awful word
That seals her doom.
Ye built her temple: shall it be her tomb?
Shall the fair promise of all foregone years
Be rapt into irrevocable gloom?
O, weigh your answer ere you let it go!
The world's best hopes, the world's worst fears
Tremble around you. Lo!
On either dim horizon Spirits twin
Attend your summons. In the shivering West.
Black on the threshold of the night,
The Spirit of wrath, the Spirit of sin,
The Spirit of blight
Uprears a lurid crest
And balances for flight :
While in the dawning far,
Where on the forehead of the crownèd Day
Flashes the Orient star,
Pluming her pinions for the downward way,
Hovers the Spirit of light,
The Spirit of love, the Spirit of sweet release,
The Spirit of God, the holy Spirit of Peace !

Memoir of Rev. George Fenwick,

HUGH CAPERTON, Esq.

LADIES AND GENTLEMEN: I beg the favor of your indulgent attention for a very few moments, during which I shall read to you a hastily prepared sketch of a distinguished scholar and an excellent Priest and Professor, late of this institution, who, I doubt not, is either personally or by reputation favorably known to most of you, and to whose admirable life and character it may not be uninteresting briefly to recur. In the constant and grateful recollections of my pupilage at old Georgetown College, where I was, for upwards of four years, from the class of Second Rudiments to the period of graduation, the favored recipient of the unvaried though undeserved kindness of the Faculty and Brotherhood of this honored institution, there is one conspicuous personage always present—always prominent—always beloved. Who that was ever cotemporaneous with him at this beautiful seat of learning and piety does not remember with emotions of inexpressible pleasure, Father George Fenwick? What reminiscences of those halcyon days passed within the classic precincts of this venerable old University are not warmed and heightened by his all-pervading spirit? When does memory ever revive the delightful scenes of our collegiate career, that he is not inseparably linked with all that gave life and light and joyousness to those scenes? There he stands, with his impressive and unmistakable features, in all of his lineaments more nearly resembling the North American Indian than the descendants of his own Saxon origin. His erect and manly figure, prominent cheek-bones, swarthy complexion and large, piercing black eyes, beaming with intelligence, fasten our attention, and mark him as a man of no ordinary character. I love to think of and talk about him, and discuss his merits. There was naught that was cold or repulsive, either in his appearance or his demeanor. On the contrary, there was such cordial salutation in his winning smile, such modest affability of manner, frankness of expression and cheerfulness of tone, that one was bound as if by a magic tie to the affections of his great, capacious heart. He won upon you from the very moment you ever saw him, and in all subsequent intercourse your captivity was but confirmed by his loving kindness and unfading sympathy. In fact, there was so much of directness and such an absence of guile in his composition that any one could read him, and after a brief acquaintance it was impossible to resist the goodness, truth and sincerity of that frank, open and *affidavit* face. His talents, erudition and scholarship, improved by the best Italian culture of many years, earned for him and entitled him to the highest consideration. His ardent zeal in promoting the substantial interests of that old College which he might almost call the place of his nativity, his love of letters, of poetry, of music, (in which he excelled,) his genial hospitality, his urbanity, his benign philosophy and uniform piety are all too well known to require an extended notice in this hasty sketch; for they rendered him distinguished amongst the many eminent of the wise and good men of this renowned institution. All who were intimately acquainted with him must have been deeply impressed with his honest zeal for learning and education, his glowing admiration of our great statesmen and orators of all parties, and his sterling and unquestioned patriotism. So thoroughly identified was he with the celebration of our national holidays, that no public ceremonies at the College on the 22d of February and 4th of July were considered complete until the soul-stirring strains of "The Star Spangled Banner," from his full, rich and magnificent tenor, aroused the throbbing pulse of freedom, and filled each heart with patriotic fire and devotion. And yet, with all of his acknowledged attainments, he was as unpretending as he was unobtrusive—as ready to impart instruction to the humblest as to hold debate with the most accomplished. But apart from these high intellectual qualities, his faculty for the management of individuals, his influence over others, his moral force, was his peculiar and distinctive characteristic. The fascinating power, the refreshing beauty, the ineffable charm of his organization was the deep, pure, fresh and ever-flowing heart-fountain of sympathy with struggling and developing youth. It was strange how one of his years and avocations, highly-cultivated mind and fondness for classic lore, could so transfuse his spirit as to become identified and incorporated with all the thoughts and hopes, whims and sorrows, fancies and disappointments, and dreams and aspirations of unreflecting and impetuous boyhood. As much as he partook of the merriment of animated youth did he sympathise with its crosses, and in many instances did his heart beat in unison with the alternate elevations and depressions of boyhood's sanguine and sensitive temperament. Though an earnest and consistent advocate for discipline and order, yet he was eminently conservative and just, and has been known in several instances to adopt the troubles of an unfortunate student who had become apparently amenable to authority, and to battle them through with a zeal and pertinacity that argued his deep conviction of innocence, or at least of great palliation of offence. The first time the author of these desultory observations remembers distinctly to have had his attention directed to him was in the year 1837, not long after he had entered college. The good priest was passing out of the large northerly building, when he was suddenly set upon with shouts of boyish delight by several urchins and two or three children of larger growth. Some were swinging around his neck, some were tugging at his cassock, one had his cap, and others secured his hands, and there was a lively scuffle, amidst the laughter and gleeful acclamations of everybody—spectators and actors. To this kind and single-hearted professor 'twas fun indeed, and I subsequently found that such playful encounters were of frequent occurrence. Who could help admiring his simplicity of nature and benignity of heart? He invited your friendly confidence, and it was never abused. In his affectionate regard there was no alloy. Never, whilst memory lasts or gratitude continues to be a virtue, can the author of this poor tribute to the virtues of his generous friend forget the deep and abiding interest he manifested in his welfare. Especially does he dwell with pleasurable sensations, though tinged with melancholy, upon his connection and that of his classmates with their thoughtful and warm-hearted preceptor, during the last two years of their academic course, through the classes of Rhetoric and Philosophy. All that the most tender regard and paternal solicitude for our instruction and happiness could accomplish was unceasingly employed in our behalf. His tact was displayed in a consummate manner in stimulating us to the most faithful application and getting out of us the greatest amount of work. No unworthy motives were encouraged, no jealous rivalry inspired, and there was no want of individual esteem between us to be deplored. A laudable desire of improvement and an honest spirit of emulation were felt and cherished by us all. In addition to the zealous care bestowed on our scholastic exercises, partial kindnesses and valued favors were judiciously conferred. If, at any time, a ramble over the adjacent hills was suggested, the pleasure of the excursion could only be enhanced by the presence of Father George. If a desire was expressed to visit either of the District cities a little oftener than the strict rule of the College required, permission was sure to be obtained, together with a more liberal supply of funds than the rigid weekly allowance of "an eleven-penny bit." Were there any lectures, discourses or exhibitions of an instructive or agreeable nature to be given in the towns, his was the ready acquiescence in accompanying us to them, or permission to go by ourselves. We were big boys—in a high class—and therefore entitled to more consideration and more privileges than the rest of the "brainless brats," as he laughingly denominated us nearly all! All these indulgences and good will were held in high estimation by us. But the chief benefaction, the crowning favor, the inestimable boon, in our carnal and unpoetical judgments, was an eloquent appeal to our stomachs, in the never-failing treat that awaited us, in his room, on our way to the dormitory from late studies. The popularity of our friend amongst all classes and denominations was such that he was liberally supplied with voluntary contributions of all kinds of edibles, and he was too skillful a caterer ever to permit our larder, (for it was exclusively appropriated to the favored four,) to become exhausted. How the love of such reward sweetened our labors! when the poetic images of Homer and Horace and Cicero were beautifully interblended with visions of sandwiches, and sardines, and oysters, and cold opossum, and roast fowl twirling before the Professor's cheerful fire with savory and appetizing odor! Those were the real "*Noctes Ambrosianæ.*" Never a partaker himself, his calm and delighted contemplation, from behind his fragrant cigar, of our enjoyment of the repast, only lent to it an additional relish. It apparently did him more good to look on than it did us to feast; but we never could have made such a concession. He was full of kindness and geniality and humor, and fond of badinage. He was never moody or ill-tempered, and whilst he found pleasure in poking fun at others, he always took a repartee or retaliation in perfectly good part. So far from being stern and exacting, he was of a gentle and forgiving nature—none had more of the milk of human kindness. The author, once, with a friend since dead, poor fellow! a young poet of fine heart and brilliant promise, by the name of Lewis, but familiarly called "Wild Horse," slipped in the afternoon from the College bounds, and soon found his way to a country tavern in the neighborhood well known as the "Students' Retreat" or the "Bull's Inn." On our return to the walks we tarried near the spring at the further end of them, when one of us suggested that we should wait until the priests' bell rang for supper before we made a further advance. It so happened that Father Fenwick and the Rev. Father McSherry, then President of the College, were passing on the opposite side of the walks, and were hidden from our view by the summer foliage. Overhearing our conversation, they made a sudden descent upon us, to our great and pitiable consternation. Upon discovering the two exemplars of propriety at such an hour and place, they seemed as much mortified as we felt, and gently admonished us to get into bounds as soon as possible. None but boys in our predicament can imagine the tumult of our feelings. There we were, checked in the midst of stolen pleasure, cut down in the height of our felicity, caught "*flagranti delicto.*" Our hearts were too big for utterance.

"Silently and sad we 'toddled' home,
And spoke not a word of sorrow,
Resolved to the Bull's Inn never to roam,
And bitterly thought of the morrow!"

The morrow came, and with it breathless anxiety. The excitement was intense, and our hearts throbbed with convulsive nervousness. The suspense seemed interminable, for it was not until the evening of the following day, when, with my face turned to the desk in the class-room, and unable to appreciate my studies, in consequence of the dread and ominous silence hitherto observed upon our case, I recognized Father George's deliberate footsteps approaching my position, and presently heard in a distinct whisper meant only for myself, and without a single word of inquiry or comment, "Wild Horse, wait until those *old* priests go into supper." A mischievous and teasing perversion of our language, it is true, but it brought instant relief. Then was a great and oppressive weight taken off my mind, and I hailed in those whispering sounds the glad tidings of forbearance and forgiveness. Next came the history of our foraging expedition to the "Bull's Inn," and how we regaled ourselves on ham and eggs, damson preserves, and Newark cider—which we bought and drank for champagne—'twas just as good. Our transgression was passed over kindly. But Father George never forgot upon meeting the author to wave his index finger and shake his head in a manner that all must certainly recollect, and exclaim—"Bull's Inn, damson preserves, and Newark cider." This is only one of a hundred examples that might be given of his mild and lenient disposition, by which he converted our very faults into arguments that made us "grapple him to our soul with hooks of steel." There was always a sly humor lurking in his significant and expressive smile, and he would every now and then indulge his jocular fancy by assuming a mysterious air with reference to our movements and chuckling over our perplexity. Thus, if by accident, or through a little sportive precaution, he had acquainted himself with our visits and wanderings in Washington or Georgetown, upon leave of absence, he would so adroitly bring the facts to our knowledge as to make us almost think—sometimes—he was the very devil himself. If he had been a very bad man instead of a very good one, and lived in latter times, what a dextrous detective he would have made. The darkest and most ingeniously concealed plottings of disloyalty would have been inevitably dragged to the public light: property deserving of instantaneous confiscation would have been infallibly recognized as if by patriotic inspiration: and Baker the peerless would have been eclipsed forever. Uncle Toby, as he was sometimes familiarly called, would always have his joke and run his rigs on some one or other, but never in a rude, disagreeable or offensive manner.

As above stated in these notes, he took a retort courteous in good temper, and was never ruffled by amiable repartee. The writer of these reminiscences once learned from him that the Sisters of the Visitation, with peculiar feminine suggestiveness, sent him a present, one day after he had been over at their convent, of a pair of razors and a shaving-brush and soap. Now when it is remembered that Father George, with all of his virtues, possessed to a remarkable degree the *vis inertiæ*—in other words that he was downright lazy (though never idle)—and that he often went unshaven for several days together, which gave him a sort of Vulcan-like appearance, the entire propriety of the above-named present will be readily appreciated. This was too good for him to keep to himself. Therefore, whenever afterwards the writer would behold the aforesaid waving finger, and hear the old speech of the "Bull's Inn, damson preserves and Newark cider," he couldn't resist the temptation to cry out, with a similar gesture—alas! alas! Uncle Toby—"Shaving-brush, razors and soap;" and he would shake all over with laughing gratification. His oddness of conceit and drollery didn't desert him even in sickness. One day during the period of the notorious Know-nothing excitement, he was lying on his bed, a silent sufferer from severe indisposition. Suddenly a favorable wind wafted the tolling sound of one of the church bells in the lower part of Georgetown. Turning to the persons in his sick-chamber, and waving the inevitable fore-finger, he interrupted his long silence by saying, with the most ludicrous gravity, "Another Know-Nothing gone to the devil," and again composed himself for quiet rest. Thus he passed through life,

"And kept the even tenor of his way,"

until his death, which occurred at the College in the month of November, 1857, in the fifty-sixth year of his age. The last time I ever beheld his amiable countenance was shortly before his demise, and when he was deprived of the power of articulation. There was electric virtue in his earnest and cordial pressure of my hand, and whilst the dying man was incapable of utterance, never can there be effaced from my memory those great, speaking, loving, eloquent eyes, and that benignant smile which appeared as a ray of light penetrating from the Home land to which he was rapidly tending, and "serenely adorning the calm eve of his life." Peace to his ashes! But if perchance the reader of this imperfect review should feel that the incidents and traits of character noted in it are dwelt upon with anything like tedious prolixity, the author craves his generous indulgence, and pleads as an apology his fervent affection and profound veneration for his deceased friend and benefactor.

Catholic Mirror's Account of the Celebration.

The grand reunion of the Alumni of Georgetown College, under the auspices of the Philodemic Society, took place at the College, on Tuesday, July 2d, in accordance with previous announcement. For some years past, the Philodemic Society has held its grand annual meetings on the anniversary of its foundation, January 17th, but that day having, for various reasons, been found inconvenient, it was decided last January to transfer the celebration to the day immediately preceding the annual commencement of the College. At the same time it was determined, in connection with the Faculty of the College, to hold a grand reunion of all the Alumni of the College on the day named. The location of the College at the seat of the General Government, and exactly midway between the Northern and Southern sections of our country, had, for many years, united in a peculiar degree, upon the rolls of its students, the names of young men from all parts of the Union, and, consequently, its Alumni were especially affected by the separating influences of the late civil contest. It was, therefore, thought worthy of a special effort to gather back, on this occasion, to their Alma Mater, as many as possible of her children, to strike hands anew amidst the blessed scenes of College life, to rekindle old friendships, bury animosities, if, perchance, such should have been engendered by the civil strife, and to go forth as in other years, a united band of brothers. To that end the officers of the Society, resident at the College, entered into a correspondence with the Alumni throughout the country, soliciting their presence and co-operation in the celebration. It was found that over six hundred names were on the list of those entitled to be present, of whom, however, one hundred and

7

fifty are known to have passed from things, of earth and uncertainty of the fate of many others, especially in view of recent events, induces the fear that the list of the departed is much longer. As even in days happier than those from which we are now emerging, the toils and tempests of life would keep away many, whose hearts inclined them towards their College homes, so it was known that still more in the desolations which now afflict many sections of our country, too many, alas! might have to deny themselves the pleasure of the reunion. But the large number of letters received from those who could not come, evinced their great concern for and fervent co-operation in the celebration, and the appointed hour beheld, gathered at the College, an assemblage fully equalling expectation. To say the meeting proved to be one of great interest, would most poorly describe it. To one not a participator in the feelings evoked by the occasion, it would be indeed difficult to represent the warm greetings of the reception, the lively gratification at the literary exercises, and the deep enthusiasm of the social reunion. The public had been invited to the literary exercises, and a large audience had early filled the Exhibition Hall, in which they were to be held. The Alumni marched in a body to the hall, and occupied the spacious platform appropriated on Commencement Day to the Students of the College. In the temporary absence of the President of the Philodemic, the chair was filled by John Carroll Brent, Esq., of Washington city, one of the early and leading graduates of the College, who has always taken a lively interest in the affairs of the Philodemic Society. The orator originally selected for the anniversary was Richard T. Merrick, Esq., of Washington city, but his engagements as counsel in the Surratt trial having unexpectedly intervened to prevent his fulfillment of the festival duty, at a late day, the Hon. Alexander Dimitry, of New Orleans, a graduate of the class of 1817, kindly consented to meet, as well as he might, the emergency. The high reputation for scholarship of this distinguished gentleman, his well-known and versatile ability, as well as his efficiency, so ably displayed in the various positions of honor occupied by him, both in the domestic and foreign service of the

United States and of his native State, gave assurance that he was in every way equal to the occasion. And most nobly did he fulfill expectation. We dare not flatter ourselves that we do even faint justice when we state, in the words of one present, that "his address was conceived and written with the best graces and fascinations of the most mature scholarship; simple in diction, chaste and elegant in its imagery; classic, tender and elevated from the beginning to the end."

His discourse occupied an hour in delivery, and its principal theme was the portrayal of the real advantages of an *education*. As we are to have the pleasure of seeing this noble production in print, we will not attempt a recital of its conclusive arguments, thrilling language, and glowing imagery. It was certainly a most triumphant vindication of the worth of that which alone raises man from the condition of a savage, and which is only depreciated by those who, possessing it not, feel not its priceless value. The respectful attention yielded to the opening of the address was soon heightened into a lively enthusiasm, which evinced its approbation by tokens that the orators of old deemed the crowning guerdon of oratory, the tribute of sympathetic tears.

Daniel A. Casserly, Esq., of New York city, a graduate of the class of 1862, and now connected with the "*Round Table*," then proceeded to deliver the poem. It was, truly, a highly finished production, lyric in form, and it took by surprise those accustomed to the poetical efforts usual on anniversary occasions. The opening lines, pronounced by the sonorous voice of the author, stirred as the sound of a trumpet, and the true poetic fire which glowed throughout the piece warmed up the attention during the entire half hour of its delivery. The subject was "War and Peace," and, although not treated in a vein calculated to give pleasure to all present, estranged as they had been in feelings during the late civil strife, it was certainly a high tribute to its polished and classic language and genuine poetic inspiration, that it elicited frequent applause even from those who might have wished its sentiments different. It is due to Mr. Casserly to say, that he kindly undertook to supply, on a few days' notice, the position which had been accorded to another gentleman, prevented by sickness from being present; and in offering for the entertainment a poem not especially prepared for the occasion, he proved in an eminent degree, not only his disposition to oblige, but the fertility of a genius ready at the instant call of his Alma Mâter to do her honor.

But the crowning feature of this delightful feast was the paper prepared and read by Hugh Caperton, Esq., of Georgetown, D. C., as a tribute to the memory of the late Father George Fenwick, a gifted and accomplished Professor of Georgetown College, who was born within the limits of the College, and died there in 1857, at the age of fifty-six years, after having devoted his life and great abilities to the promotion of literature, science and virtue within those classic walls. The writer had been a favorite pupil of Father Fenwick, and portrayed his noble and saint-like character in a vein of mingled humor and pathos that took captive the ears and hearts of all. Seldom can it be our privilege to listen to such a loving and truthful delineation, and we know not whether most to envy the speaker the possession of such a friend, or the ability to render such justice and honor to his memory.

The intervals between the exercises were enlivened by music from the College Band ; and after the conclusion of the literary entertainment, there was held a meeting of the Philodemic Society for the transaction of business. This was private; but there can be no impropriety in saying that delight at the grand success of the reunion just concluded found vent in fervent congratulations, and seemed to animate all with renewed zeal for the promotion of the prosperity of the society and the College.

Next succeeded the more material feast of the day—the dinner. Although imperative duty compelled some to leave immediately after the reading of the memoir, a procession computed to number more than one hundred and fifty passed to the "boys' refectory," where the long tables spread with an abundant banquet awaited them. Father Maguire, the President of the College, presided. After invoking a blessing, the company was seated, and it was then observed that, almost without seeming concert, the members of the different graduating classes had managed to get together in renewal of their former assemblage around the same tables. The first sight that greeted the eye was the "bill of fare." This had been gotten up in classic style, and was headed by the following pleasing salutation:

"Her children coming back to their boyhood's home, not with costly viands and courtly delicacies, but with the invigorating repast that made them lithe and strong of limb in their young, heroic days, old Georgetown welcomes!"

"Think oft, ye brethren;
Think of the gladness of our youthful prime—
It cometh now again, that golden time!"
German Student's Song.

To this, followed a list of viands and wines, which showed that the "invigorating repast" was something more than what is ordinarily understood by "College commons," for it comprehended all the essentials of a first-class dinner. The name of each dish was followed by a quotation from Shakespeare, the appositeness of which evinced not a little taste and research. The solid part of the dinner was then duly appreciated. On the removal of the cloth Father Maguire arose, and with that cordiality of address, warmth of manner, and force of expression, for which he is so remarkable, spoke of his great gratification at the presence of so many of the children of the College, and renewed publicly the cheering welcome which, during the day, he had privately extended to each comer. He spoke at some length, and with his usual felicity, of "school-boy days," and the pleasant hours and scenes thereof, and hoped the happy reunion might be the beginning of a series of annual meetings of the Alumni and old students of the College. He mentioned the fact that just fifty years had elapsed since the first class had graduated at Georgetown, and although the idea of the celebration had originated without reference to this circumstance, no less interest would attach to it from its being the semi-centennial anniversary. He concluded by remarking that as his first task had been to welcome those present, his next should be the recollection of those who had been unable to attend, and he therefore proposed the health of the absent Alumni and members of the Philodemic Society. After due honor had been done to the toast, Father Maguire said that in that connection he would call on Mr. Hoffman, the chairman of the committee of invitation, who had in charge the correspondence pertaining thereto.

Mr. Hoffman made some interesting statements in regard to the number of the Alumni and members of the Society, the list of the departed, and other facts developed by the correspondence. He mentioned that he had received a very large number of letters of a highly interesting character from those whose engagements had prevented them from being present, all breathing fervent wishes for the success of the celebration; and as, in conformity with the request of the circular of invitation, each of these letters contained a sentiment for the consideration of the festival, he had, the night before, arranged the toasts and letters in order to read them at the dinner. But it happened that very many who did not come in person, in the hope, perhaps, of being able to do so, deferred their replies until the last moment, and hence he had received a large package of letters that morning which he had barely time to read, and a still larger package came by the mail at noon, which had not yet even been opened. Under these circumstances he had deemed it wiser not to read the letters and sentiments on that occasion, as all, though equally deserving of attention, could not possibly receive it. He had, therefore, resolved to have them placed in such a form as to make them accessible to all the members, which was understood to be their publication in due time, along with the oration, the memoir and the poem. He also desired to state that in compliance with another request of the circular of invitation, nearly all the letters of reply contained the photographs of their writers, endorsed as desired; that most of the gentlemen present had already given in theirs also, and he therefore hoped that those who had as yet neglected the matter would likewise comply as soon as possible, as an album had been prepared for the reception of the photographs, and he was happy to be able to say that this promised to be one of the most successful features of the celebration.

He then read one letter, as it was from a member of the first graduating class of the College in the year 1817. It was a warm-hearted letter, giving an account of the condition of the College at the time the writer was a student there, and also the names of the professors and many of the students of the time, all of whom, as far as known, have departed, except the venerable Father John McElroy, who was then Treasurer of the College. The writer was a native of England, and came to the College from New York city, where his father then resided, but he subsequently settled in the South, and for many years has been a banker at Augusta, Ga. A call was made for the reading of a letter understood to have been received from General Lee. It was his response to the invitation extended him as a member of the Philodemic, expressing his friendly greeting to the members, and his warm wishes for the success of the festival. This letter had been addressed to Rev. James Clarke, President of the Society, as Father C. had been the General's classmate, having graduated at the same time with him at West Point. Calls were made for Father Clarke, but he being absent, Father Maguire asked for the reading of at least one of the sentiments of the absent members in response to the toast in their honor. Mr. Hoffman expressed his gratification that the first one on which his eye rested should be so appropriate. It was the sentiment of Robert Ray, Esq., of Monroe, La. "The Jesuit Society, Followers of Jesus, Teachers of Youth! Their schools inspire a veneration for the Christian Religion, and a high esteem for our Republican Form of Government." Father Maguire then proposed, as next in order, the health of the orator, poet, and biographer of the day, which was honored and responded to in turn by each of those gentlemen. The sentiments and remarks then became more informal, and for a long time engaged and delighted the company. Conspicuous among the good things elicited was the recitation of a brief poem by Charles B. Kenny, Esq., of Pittsburg, Pa., as an embodiment of the sentiments suggested by the reunion; a most amusing medley of German and English in a song, by James D. Dougherty, of Harrisburg, Pa., and a neat and eloquent speech from R. R. Crawford, Esq., ex-Mayor of Georgetown, picturing the reverses which had visited the College during the war, and describing with exultation its rapid recuperation to the point of its former prosperity now already attained. Many other gentlemen entertained the company with their eloquence and wit, and thus the hours wore pleasantly away until the approach of night suggested the closing exercises. Appended to the bill of fare was a song written for the occasion and arranged to the tune of "Auld Lang Syne." The entire company arose, and with united voice and swelling hearts fervently sang the words which will long be recollected as the closing scene of this rare and memorable reunion of the students of Georgetown College.

The Bill of Fare.

Her Children, coming back to their Boyhood's Home,

Not with costly viands and courtly delicacies, but with the invigorating repast that made them lithe and strong of limb in their young, heroic days,

OLD GEORGETOWN WELCOMES!

Think oft, ye brethren;
Think of the gladness of our youthful prime—
It cometh now again, that golden time!
German Student's Song.

Bill of Fare, (a la Shakespeare.)

Soup St. Julian.
" Expect spoon-meat."

Brisket Beef.
" Chief nourisher in life's feast."

Boiled Chickens with Oyster Sauce.
" You would eat chickens in the shell."

Smoked Tongue.
" This is the vein which makes flesh a deity."

Sliced Ham.
" I should time expend with such a slice."

Roast Beef.
" Daylight and champagne discover not better."

Veal Sweetbread.
" Veal," quoth the Dutchman, " is not veal a calf?"

8

New Potatoes.
" Let the sky rain potatoes." "From the still vexed Bermoothes."

Asparagus.
"A green goddess."

Green Peas.
" I had rather have a handful or two of pease."

Maryland Lettuce.
" We may pick a thousand salads,
Ere we light on such another herb."

Beets, Cucumbers, Tomatoes.
" Will do well in such a shift."

French Olives.
" To thee the heavens adjudge the olive."

College Pies, Cakes, &c.
" The fruits are to ensue."
"And any pretty, little, tiny kickshaws."

Tutti-Frutti Ice Cream.
" Tut, tut, thou art all ice, thy kindness freezes."

Raisins, Prunes, Oranges, Nuts, &c.
" Your pounds of prunes, and as many raisins of the sun."
" Give this orange to your friend."
"And fetch the new nuts."
" The fig of Spain, very good."

Wines, &c.
" Go, fetch me a quart of sack; put a toast in it."

Monody on Hash.*

I.
There is not in this wide world a viand so sweet,
As the hash that's concocted of all sorts of meat:
Oh! the comb with its honey'll be bitter and tart,
Ere the taste of that hash from my mouth shall depart.

II.
Yet it was not that *Derks* had spread o'er the dish
The sauces of Soyer, or lobster, or fish;
'Twas not the vile gravy we every day swill;
Oh! no, it was something more exquisite still.

* Hash—a *sine qua non* of the College breakfast table.

III.

'Twas *onions*, delight of my stomach, I found
In plenteous abundance were swimming around;
And I felt how the best kind of hash may improve,
When to onions is added a taste of the clove.

IV.

Sweet hash of old Georgetown! how calm could I rest,
With a dose of that mixture inside of my vest!
No nightmare approaches, disturbing one's peace,
As after a supper of canvass-back geese.

V.

The Romans might boast of their nightingale brains,
And tongues of the peacock, and gizzards of cranes;
The Chinese may gobble their rats and their mice,
And imagine these vermin exceedingly nice;

VI.

The Dutchman may swallow his lager and kraut—]
The Russian his candle, quite pleasant no doubt—
But in my estimation such tit-bits are trash,
When compared with a dishful of onions and hash.

SONG.

(Written for the occasion, to be sung by the whole Company.)

I.

Should old acquaintance be forgot,
And never brought to mind?
Should old acquaintance be forgot,
And the days of auld lang syne?

CHORUS:—
For days of auld lang syne, my friends,
For days of auld lang syne,
We'll speak a word of kindness yet,
For days of auld lang syne.

II.

In boyhood days we oft have met
Around this hallow'd shrine:
Tho' years have pass'd, we ne'er forget
Those hours of auld lang syne.

CHORUS:—Those hours, &c.

III.

Since then we've seen both time and war
　With ruthless hand combine.
To sever wide and scatter far
　The friends of auld lang syne.
　　　Chorus:—The friends, &c.

IV.

And even 'neath this peaceful shade,
　Grim Mars, with fierce design,
Did dare to enter and invade
　Our home of auld lang syne.
　　　Chorus:—Our home, &c.

V.

But now 'tis over, and once more
　Our yearning hearts incline
Our steps from many a distant shore,
　Towards scenes of auld lang syne.
　　　Chorus:—Towards scenes, &c.

VI.

And as in days of youthful joys,
　Our hands once more entwine—
We see the face, we hear the voice
Of happy auld lang syne.
　　　Chorus:—Of happy, &c.

VII.

But whilst we greet with glowing heart,
　Let memory enshrine
The many absent, who are part
Of days of auld lang syne.
　　　Chorus:—Of days, &c.

VIII.

Then, ere we sever, let us raise
　One fervent cup of wine,
In mem'ry of the happy days
　And friends of auld lang syne.
　　　Chorus:—And friends, &c.

For the Reunion at Georgetown College,

JULY 2, 1867.

BY CHARLES B. KENNY.

Alma Mater, our love, without censure or stain,
Behold in thy bosom thy children again !
From the great world of passion, of grasping and strife,
We come with the scars of the battle of life ;
We come to affirm, with the judgment of men,
The lessons of youth you enjoined on us then ;
And gratefully prove the affection and pride
That in sons of a noble old mother abide.
No Phæthon here with a querulous tongue,
And soul with distrust and uncertainty stung,
To charge, with a brow where opprobrium rests,
That his thought-life was drawn from adulterate breasts,
And dare to control, whilst authority chides,
The radiant car that intelligence guides—
No Renau or Colenso, with impious pen,
To wound our old faith in the Savior of men,
And drive a god's car, with presumptuous soul,
In a purposeless flight without beacon or goal,
Till prone from the wrath of Omnipotence hurled,
With ruin and wreck to himself and the world.
But thy teachings, good mother, one maxim imply—
"For God and our country to live or to die."
O brothers ! may never His footstool again
See the Demon of Discord so cruelly reign ;
May the land that we love, and the nations applaud,
No more feel the scourge of the justice of God !
No more, till the last of mortality's flood,
May brothers lie crimsoned with mutual blood !
That is past—and the angel of peace has returned
Where "the fire-shower of ruin" remorselessly burned ;
Arts, commerce and science, like sunbeams, relume
The scenes that Mars pall'd with his deadliest gloom ;
Now olive-crowned Clio exults in her wreath,
And Melpomone's dagger is red in its sheath,

The Jove-fathered sisters smile sweetly serene—
But their mother still weeps for the days that have been.
Oh! how priceless are now the firm friendships of youth,
That spring from its candor, its fervor and truth;
How sweet to unite where fond memories rest,
And feel the old throb of our mother's warm breast;
Where mingled love's ties that no fortune could chill,
And the horrors since witness'd make tenderer still!
Though diverse in fortune, faith, climate and race,
Our bosoms are one in our mother's embrace;
They are one till remembrance and life shall depart,
And charity dwell in no Catholic heart.
Here the sons of the old Philodemic renew
The friendships young life to its confidence drew;
Here they pledge their old love to their cherishing mother,
To be true to her teaching and true to each other;
Thus may mother and children, in unison still,
For God and our country their mission fulfill,
And long may His love, in true brotherhood, save
The land of the free and the home of the brave!

Mr. Barber's Letter.

AUGUSTA, GA., *June* 21, 1867.

REVEREND AND DEAR SIR:

I have before me a copy of your circular of April 15, addressed to the former students of Georgetown College. It would give me great pleasure to attend the Celebration on the 2d July next, but confinement to a sick bed will render that impossible. Although not a member of the Philodemic Society, as no such society existed during my connection with the College, I send you my photograph as requested, and proceed to give you a few memoranda concerning myself, which I trust may not prove uninteresting, most especially should there be at your Celebration any who were students at the same time with myself. I have to trust entirely to memory, having no written memoranda to guide me, and after the lapse of so many years, it may not be surprising if I am sometimes incorrect as to dates. I entered Georgetown College some time during the year 1814 : I had been a student at the "New York Literary Institution," presided over by the Rev. Benedict Fenwick, afterwards Bishop of Boston, assisted by Prof. James Wallace, (afterwards Reverend.) Upon the closing of that institution I went to Georgetown, accompanied by Prof. Wallace, and some other students, among whom I recollect Charles and George Dinies, Henry Riley, Dennis Doyle, and —— Skiddy.

Rev. John Grassi was President of the College, and James Wallace Professor of Mathematics.

The principal teachers were Thomas Downing, John Kelley, and James Murphy; Mr. John McElroy (now Reverend) was Procurator of the College. James Rider was my class-mate, and among my fellow-students were George Fenwick, Charles C. Pise, and Thomas Mullady.

I was at the College when the British troops entered Washington, and I witnessed the destruction of the public buildings. Some time after the close of the war, Mr. Baxter (afterwards Reverend) came from Stonehurst, England, and became a Professor in the College. Classes were re-arranged and I became one of the Senior Class, together with Charles and George Dinies, Edward Bergh, of New York, and Stephen Henry Gough, of Port Tobacco, Md.

This was the first class which graduated. I went to New York, where my parents resided, for a short visit, intending to return immediately to complete my course of studies, but was prevented by the sudden death of my father ; I therefore did not receive my diploma with the other members of the class.

Previous to the formation of this class, Mr. Rider, Mr Pise and Mr. G. Fenwick had entered their novitiate, or gone to Rome. I think I left the College in 1817, when Rev. Benedict Fenwick became President, which will give you the precise date, if I am in error.

After a residence of some years in New York, Charleston, S. C., and Columbia, S. C., I settled in this city, fifteen years ago, and am the senior of the firm of F. C.

Barber & Son, Bankers and Brokers. These few memoranda, hastily thrown together, I feel are very imperfect, as I have been for some months confined to a bed of sickness and great suffering; but I could not deny myself the pleasure of noticing your kind invitation.

I have the honor, dear sir, to be,

Most respectfully,

Your obedient servant,

FREDERICK C. BARBER.

Rev. B. A. Maguire, *Georgetown College, D. C.*

LIST OF MEMBERS

OF THE

Philodemic Society of Georgetown College, D. C.

RESIDENT MEMBERS.

CHARLES S. ABELL, Maryland.
WALTER R. ABELL, Maryland.
GABRIEL BUSTAMENTI, Mexico.
JOHN CLEVELAND, South Carolina.
N. CALVIN COLLIER, Georgia.
MICHAEL E. GRIFFIN, Connecticut.
WILLIAM A. HAMMOND, Virginia.

FRANK C. KIECKHOEFER, D. C.
D. CLINTON LYLES, Maryland.
STEPHEN R. MALLORY, Florida.
WILLIAM O'BRIEN, New York.
LOUIS C. PUEBLA, Mexico.
HENRY A. SEYFERT, Pennsylvania.
WILLIAM J. NICHOLSON, D. C.

NON-RESIDENT MEMBERS.

GRADUATES.

Rev. SAMUEL A. MULLEDY, Virginia.
EUGENE A. LYNCH, Maryland.
JOHN C. BRENT, Dist. Columbia.
GEORGE BRENT, Maryland.
Rev. WILLIAM F. CLARKE, Baltimore.
REUBEN CLEARY, Louisiana.
DANIEL C. DIGGES, Maryland.
Rev. GEORGE FENWICK, Mass.
Maj. ED. FITZGERALD, U. S. A.
BENJ. R. FLOYD, Virginia.
E. M. MILLARD, Louisiana.
Rev. CHAS. H. STONESTREET, Md.
JAMES McSHERRY, Virginia.
THOS. H. KENNEDY, Louisiana.
DANIEL J. DESMOND, Pennsylvania.
LEWIS W. JENKINS, Maryland.
WILLIAM GWYN, Maryland.
S. H. GOUGH, Maryland.
EDWARD A. LYNCH, Maryland.

W. R. GREEN, Dist. Columbia.
Hon. ALEX. DIMITRY, Louisiana.
Hon. CHAS. J. FAULKNER, Virginia.
Hon. SOLO HILLEN, Maryland.
Rev. C. CONSTANTINE PISE, D. D.
Dr. ELCON A. JONES, D. C.
R. D. CUTTS, District of Columbia.
Rev. ED. A. HASTINGS, Georgetown College, District of Columbia.
EDWARD DOYLE, New York.
Dr. P. H. HAMILTON, Maryland.
WILLIAM R. HARDING, Maryland.
NICHOLAS STONESTREET, Maryland.
THOMAS PRESTON, Virginia.
P. PEMBERTON MORRIS, Pennsylvania.
Rev. THOS. M. JENKINS, Maryland.
Rev. JOHN M. AIKEN, Tennessee.
LAURANT J. SEGUR, Louisiana.
PETER E. BONFORD, Virginia.

GRADUATES–Continued.

HENRY H. H. STRAWBRIDGE, La.

JOHN T. DOYLE, New York.

Prof. J. A. RITCHE, M. D., D. C.

Dr. JAMES T. LAPHEN, D. C.

Lieut. JULIUS GARASCHE, U. S. A.

GEORGE CUYLER, Georgia.

J. H. FRENCH, Virginia.

ROBERT FORD, Maryland.

BEN. E. GREEN, Dist. Columbia.

OLIVER A. LUCCETT, Georgia.

JOSHUA NICHOLAS, Dist. Columbia.

ANDREW V. VANEL, Louisiana.

WILLIAM H. LEWIS, Tennesee.

Capt. WM. S. WALKER, Mississippi.

THOS. R. JENKINS, Maryland.

JOHN H. O'NEAL, Ohio.

JOHN M. HEARD, Maryland.

HENRY J. LANG, Georgia,

GEORGE B. CLARKE, Baltimore.

JOSEPH JOHNSON, Mississippi.

Hon. T. J. SEMMES, New Orleans, La.

JAMES P. EDMONSON, Virginia.

JAMES H. BEVANS, Maryland.

WILLIAM M. BRADFORD, Georgia.

Rev. SAMUEL L. LILLY, S. J., Pa.

JOHN C. THOMPSON, Georgia.

Rev. W. D. McSHERRY, Virginia.

JOHN L. KIRKPATRICK, Georgia.

EUGENE COMMISKY, Maryland.

EDWARD DONNELLY, New York.

RICHARD H. CLARKE, D. C.

JAMES A. EIGLHART, Maryland.

WILLIAM BIERD, Georgia.

WALTER S. COX, Dist. Columbia.

FRANCIS H. DYKERS, New York.

JOHN W. ARCHER, Virginia.

ROBERT E. DOYLE, New York.

JOHN E. WILSON, Maryland.

PROSPER R. LANDRY, Louisiana.

ELIEL S. WILSON, Maryland.

L. T. BRIEN, Maryland.

Hon. WILLIAM P. BROOKE, Md.

NICHOLAS KNIGHTON, Maryland.

GEORGE MARSHALL, Tennessee.

WALDEMAR de BODISCO, Russia.

Dr. A. J. SEMMES, District of Columbia.

EOLEVIRA ANDREWS, Virginia.

JOHN. C. LONGSTRETH, Pennsylvania.

JAMES H. DONEGAN, Alabama.

CHARLES de BLANC, Louisiana.

EDMUND RUEL SMITH. New York.

HENRY J. FORSTALL, Louisiana.

ALEXANDER A. ALLEMONG, S. C.

Dr. JNO. C. RILEY, Dist. of Columbia.

BERNARD G. CAULFIELD, Dist, of Col.

LOUIS V. LANDRY, Louisiana.

CASIMER G. DESSAULES, L. Canada.

EDMUND L. SMITH, Pennsylvania.

EDMUND DESLONDE, Louisiana.

PIERRE D. D. DELACROIX, Louisiana.

Dr. ALFONSO T. SEMMES, Miss.

Dr. ADRIAN B. LEPRETE, Louisiana.

J. WILLIE RICE, Maryland.

RICHARD H. BRYAN, Maryland.

LOUIS DECOUTEULX, New York.

F. MATHEWS LANCASTER, Maryland.

LAFAYETTE J. CARRIEL, Louisiana.

CLARKE KOONTZ, Maryland.

WILLIAM X. WILLIS, Maryland.

JOHN C. C. HAMILTON, D. C.

DOMINICK A. O'BRYAN, Georgia.

EDWIN F. KING, District of Columbia.

ROBERT. W. HARPER, Maryland.

THOMAS B. KING, District of Columbia.

JOHN KING, District of Columbia.

JULIUS A. CHOPPIN, Louisiana.

JOHN K. GLEESON, Louisiana.

HENRY W. BRENDT, Maryland.

JOHN W. GRAHAM, Virginia.

ENOCH M. LOWE, Virginia.

EDWARD DESLONDE, Louisiana.

ORLANDO BROWN, Tennessee.

WILLIAM J. BOARMAN, Maryland.

WILFRED B. FETTERMAN, Pennsylvania.

THOMAS B. BOONE, District of Columbia.

JESSE F. CLEVELAND, South Carolina.

WILLIAM M. SMITH, Pennsylvania.

WILLIAM H. DUNCAN, Alabama.

BENEDICT J. SEMMES, Maryland.

PETER McGARY, Virginia.

JOSEPH P. CALLANEN, New York.

JAMES P. DONNELLY, New York.

GRADUATES- Continued.

P. C. LAROCHE, Pennsylvania.

FRANCIS CONLY, Massachusetts.

FRANCIS W. BABY, Canada.

GEORGE W. FULMER, Dist. of Columbia.

ROBERT RAY, Louisiana.

JULES D. la CROIX, Louisiana.

HARVEY BAWTREE, Vermont.

JOSEPH H. BLANDFORD, Maryland.

WILSON J. WALTHALL.

DUGENE LONGUEMARE.

JOHN J. BEALL.

FREDERICK SMITH.

J. CLEVELAND.

G. ARCAND.

L. BARGY, District of Columbia.

W. H. GWYNN.

E. M. TAUZIN, Louisiana.

R. C. COMBS, Maryland.

A. H. LOUGHBOROUGH, Dist. of Columbia.

L. L. ARMANT, Louisiana.

R. H. GARDINER, Maryland.

A. BECNEL, Louisiana.

H GASTON, Louisiana.

ALFRED F. HULLIHEN.

MANFRED F. HULLIHEN.

EDMUND ZANE.

EDWARD WILCOX.

JAMES SPELLISSY.

JOHN F. CALLAN, District of Columbia.

JOHN REICKLEMAN.

HENRY BOWLING, Maryland.

WILLIAM CHOICE, South Carolina.

W. J. HILL, Maryland.

E. ROST. Louisiana.

E. DIGGES, Maryland.

F. A. LANCASTER, Pennsylvania.

W. N. SANDERS, Maryland.

M. GARCIA de ZUNIGA, Uraguay.

C. A. HOYT, New York.

J. D. DOUGHERTY, Pennsylvania.

N. S. HILL, Maryland.

C. J. O'FLYNN, Maryland.

C. B. KENNEY, Pennsylvania.

C. C. MAGRUDER, Maryland.

SAMUEL A. ROBINSON, Dist. of Columbia.

JAMES A. WISE, District of Columbia.

EDWARD WOOTTON, Maryland.

JAMES F. McLAUGHLIN, Virginia.

HENRY W. CLAGETT.

BEVERLY C. KENNEDY, Louisiana.

ROBERT F. LOVELACE, Louisiana.

PHILIP A. MADAN, Cuba.

JAMES O. MARTIN, Louisiana.

JAMES P. NEALE, Maryland.

FRANCIS X. WARD, Maryland.

ROBERT Y. BROWN, Miss.

PAUL BOSSIER, Louisiana.

PLACIDE BOSSIER, Louisiana.

P. S. BRAND, Louisiana.

L. A. BUARD, Louisiana.

JOHN B. GARDINER, Maryland.

JOHN W. KIDWELL, D. C.

CLEMENT S. LANCASTER, Penn.

JOHN P. MARSHALL, Maryland.

A. W. NEALE, Maryland.

ANATOLE LANDRY, Louisiana.

MICHAEL A. STRONG, Pennsylvania.

FRANK RUDD, Virginia.

GABRIEL A. TOURNET, La.

LASSALINE P. BRIANT, La.

W. S. SNOW, New York.

WILLIAM H. BARRETT, Georgia.

ISAAC PAISONS, Va.

W. BERESFORD CAIR, La.

DANIEL A. CASSERLY, N. Y.

P. A. LAMBERT, D. C.

WALTER S. McFARLAN, D. C.

JOHN M. K. DAVIS, D. C.

JOHN D. O'BRYAN, Pa.

HENRY L. McCULLOUGH, Pa.

WILLIAM L. WIRST, Pa.

THOMAS M. HENAN, New Grenada.

R. ROSS PERRY, D. C.

CUPRIANO ZEGANA, Penn.

HENRY MAJOR, D. C.

JOSEPH A. RICE, La.

VUGIL F. DOMURGUES, Cuba.

CHAS. L. HEISMAN, Pa.

DANIEL H. LAFFERTY, Pa.

J. P. McELROY, N. Y.

J. H. MURPHY, N. Y.

EDWARD S. REILY, Pa.

GRADUATES—Continued.

W. F. WILLIAMS, D. C.

G. S. RUDD, Ky.

W. TAZWELL FOX, Va.

J. T. FITZPATRICK, Ala.

JOSEPH FOREST, D. C.

F. P. S. LAFFERTY, Pa.

JNO. C. WILSON, D. C.

L. P. GOULEY, N. Y.

EDWARD McCAHILL, N. Y.

R. M. DOUGLASS, Illinois.

SAMUEL H. ANDERSON, Md.

ARTHUR LEE, Md.

GEORGE H. FOX, N. Y.

JUAN H. PIZZINI, Va.

MICHAEL HALL, Ireland.

C. C. HOMER, Md.

BLADEN FORREST, D. C.

HUGH CAPERTON, D C.

SUB-GRADUATES.

JOHN H. HUNTER, Maryland.

JOHN H. DIGGES, Maryland.

JOHN R. BROOKE, Maryland.

JOHN D. K. CASHEN, Florida.

GEORGE A. DIGGES, Maryland.

THOMAS T. GANTT, Maryland.

T. S. LEE HORSEY, Delaware.

HENRY HUNTER, Maryland.

JOHN S. HURST, Virginia.

JOSEPH JENKINS, Maryland.

R. H. LIVINGSTON, New York.

EDWARD C. PRESTON, Virginia.

ANDREW K. SANDERS, Virginia.

BENJAMIN SMITH, Louisiana.

CHARLES SMITH, Louisiana.

RICHARD N. SNOWDEN, Maryland.

JAMES STEWART, Virginia.

F. W. THORNTON, Virginia.

W. R. TURNER, District Columbia.

THOMAS MATHEWS, Maryland.

Rev. J. J. BALFE, Pennsylvania.

JAMES HOLLIHAN, Pennsylvania.

FRANKLIN K. BECK, Alabama.

RICHARD B. LLOYD, Dist. Columbia.

WILLIAM H. DUNKINSON, Md.

J. ARISTIDE LANDRY, Louisiana.

WILLIAM A. LENOX, District Columbia.

WILLIAM MATHEWS MERRICK, Md.

LEWIS F. BUNDY, Louisiana.

ADAM WEAVER, Virginia.

EDMUND MENARD, Illinois.

WILLIAM D. DIGGES, Maryland.

JAMES FAYE, District Columbia.

GEORGE R. C. FLOYD, Virginia.

BEN. J. BORDEN, Upper Canada.

WILLIAM D. WILLIS, Virginia.

JOSEPH HOBAN, District Columbia.

Rev. HENRY HOBAN, District Columbia.

HENRY QUEEN, District Columbia.

WALTER MEADE THOMPSON, Md.

EDMUND J. PLOWDEN, Maryland.

NICHOLAS DIMITRY, Louisiana.

MICHAEL F. RODDY, South Carolina.

WILLIAM J. BERRY, District Columbia.

Dr. JOHN JACKSON, Virginia.

Col. THOMAS A. MAGUIRE, Penn.

Rev. JOHN A. McGUIAN, Penn.

C. B. KIERNAN, Alabama.

ONESIME GUIDRY, Louisiana.

THOMAS B. MULLEN, Pennsylvania.

JONATHAN BUTCHER, D. Columbia.

THOMAS RICHIE, Virginia.

JAMES O'REILLY, District Columbia.

JOSEPH R. PEARSON, District Columbia.

W. H. WARD, District Columbia.

P. A. LAMOTHE, Lower Canada.

Dr. JAMES A. HIGGINS, Maryland.

THOMAS J. HUNGERFORD, Virginia.

FLEMING GARDNER, Virginia.

GEORGE T. ANDREWS, East Florida.

ADONIS PETIT, Louisiana.

Col. W. W. LORING, U. S. A., Florida,

THOMAS J. CALLAHAN, Ireland.

R. M. LUSHER, South Carolina.

LYCURGUS C. VALDENER, Maryland.

RICHARD H. HAGNER, District Columbia.

JOHN G. PEYTON, Virginia.

GEORGE R. C. PRICE, Virginia.

SUB-GRADUATES—Continued.

JOSEPH G. CHEVALIE, Virginia.
DAVID WADE, Virginia.
WILLIAM H. FITZHUGH, Virginia.
R. B. GOOCH, Virginia.
Hon. HENRY A. EDMONSON, Virginia.
WILLIAM MITCHELL, Maryland.
NICHOLAS E. CLEARY, Virginia.
Dr. WILLIAM J. DIGGES, Maryland.
Dr. EDWARD A. PYE, Maryland.
TOBIAS T. DURNEY, Pennsylvania.
JOHN H. C. MUDD, Maryland.
MICHAEL WALLACE, Virginia.
JOSEPH W. KENT, Virginia.
IGN. A. LANCASTER, District Columbia.
O. A. RENTHROP, Louisiana.
LINDSEY C. WARREN, Georgia.
WILLIAM C. TAYLOR, Missouri.
Dr. ALEXIS C. GUIDRY, Louisiana.
ROBERT P. KENNY, Virginia.
WINFIELD S. GIBSON, Mississippi.
H. CARRINGTON WATKINS, Virginia.
JOHN W. TONGUE, District Columbia.
DANIEL W. ADAMS, Mississippi.
W. H. CAMPBELL, Georgia.
ZENON LEDOUX, Louisiana.
SAMUEL B. GRAHAM, South Carolina.
VIRGINIUS NEWTON, Virginia.
D. BRENT, Maryland.
CONSTANTINE DOYLE, Nova Scotia.
FRANCIS KERNAN, New York.
R. U. HYATT, District Columbia.
GEORGE C. MORGAN, Maryland.
BENJAMIN GWYNN, Maryland.
BENJAMIN YOUNG, Maryland.
PEREGRINES BUCKINGHAM.
JAMES FITTON, Virginia.
ALEXANDER CAMPAU, Michigan.
SHERIDAN MILES, Maryland.
JOHN KENNY, Virginia.
WILLIAM D. WYNN, Georgia.
HENRY B. THOMPSON, Georgia.
JOSEPH L. BRENT, Louisiana.
JOHN B. BROOKE, Jr., Maryland.
G. De LANAUDIERE, Canada.
MARTIN KENNEDY, Louisiana.
ALONZO B. DUFOUR, Georgia.

BENJAMIN E. WHALAN, Alabama.
P. F. DRAIN, District Columbia.
HENRY D. POWER, Dist. Columbia.
ALCIDE P. BUARD, Louisiana.
HENRY WILLIAMSON, Georgia.
MR. KUITON, Canada.
FELIX METOYER, Louisiana.
JAMES MASICOTT, Louisiana.
FRANCIS H. HALL, Maryland.
NICHOLAS SNOWDEN, Maryland.
JOHN SEMMES, Mississippi.
RICHARDSON DAVIS, Virginia.
J. W. POINDEXTER, Virginia.
ALBERT ERSKINE, Alabama.
POLYCARPE FORTIER, Louisiana.
HENRY A. WADE, Pennsylvania.
GEORGE LOYALL, Virginia.
WILLIAM H. BYRD, Virginia.
JULIEN CUMMIN, Georgia.
CLEMENT COX, District Columbia.
JOSEPH YOUNG, District Columbia.
ALFRED J. HIGGINS, Virginia.
WILLIAM MOUTON, Louisiana.
WILLIAM H. MOORE, Mississippi.
JAMES A. TILLMAN, Alabama.
THOMAS M. JENKINS, Maryland.
HENRY M. BEDFORD, New York.
RICHARD WELSH, Maryland.
HENRY M. BEDFORD, New York.
RICHARD WELSH, Maryland.
HERMOGENE A. DUFRENE, Louisiana.
JOHN S. RUDD, Virginia.
JOHN B. WILLS.
WILLIAM WIRT TILLEY, Dist. Col.
ZENON FREIRE, Chili, S. A.
MANUEL F. ALDUNATE, S. A.
FREDERICO ALBUNATE, S. A.
HENRY B. TRICOU, Louisiana.
WILLIAM F. GASTON, North Carolina.
C. J. MEUX, Louisiana.
JOHN McMANUS, Maryland.
ALFRED S. JAMES, Alabama.
WILLIAM E. RICHARD, Alabama.
DAVID M. CLARK, South Carolina.
PAUL BRES, Louisiana.
JAMES E. S. HARVEY, Maryland.

SUB-GRADUATES—Continued.

THOMAS M. BLOUNT, Florida.
JAMES McSHANE, Ireland.
A. S. GARNETT.
DOM. GARDINER.
J. H. S. HAMILTON.
J. W. PRESCOTT.
S. B. SMITH.
H. WOOTON, Maryland.
EDWARD SCOTT.
L. A. GRENEAUX, Louisiana.
C. E. GRENEAUX, Jr., Louisiana.
JOHN P. BOWLING, Maryland.
W. H. BLANDFORD, Maryland.
JAMES R. RANDALL.
OTIS KEIHOLTZ.
GEORGE C. HUBBARD.
J. J. GARNETT, Virginia.
LEOPOLD J. SMITH, Louisiana.
CHARLES BENOIST, Louisiana.
ARISTIDE L. AUBERT, Alabama.
CONSTANT SMITH, District Columbia.
JOHN E. YOUNG, Maryland.
A. H. HUGUET, Louisiana.
W. C. WALSH.
E. L. DECHAPELLES, Louisiana.
W. J. CLARKE, Georgia.
WILLIAM F. KELLEY, Pennsylvania.
F. A. PRICE, Georgia.
E. BOYD FAULKNER, Virginia.
C. E. O'SULLIVAN, New York.
JOSEPH P. ORME, District Columbia.
HENRY S. FOOTE, California.
HENRY CRUZAT, Louisiana.
MADISON R. GRIGSBY, Mississippi.
THEODORE J. DIMITRY, Louisiana.

JAMES L. O'BYRNE, Georgia.
WILLIAM HODGES, Mississippi.
WILLIAM N. ROACH, District Columbia.
ALFRED G. THOMSON, Louisiana.
DOMINGO FORO, Chili.
Rev. THOMAS F. MULLEDY, Virginia.
Rev. JAMES RYDER, ex-President of
    Georgetown College.
Dr. MAURICE A. POWER, New York.
Dr. ROBERT A. DURKEE, Maryland.
ROBERT BARRY, District Columbia.
Dr. P. WARFIELD, District Columbia.
Hon. T. D'AZAMBUJA, Portugal.
McCLINTOCK YOUNG, District Columbia.
HUGH McLAUGHLIN, Maryland.
J. E. DOOLY, Va.
T. B. FENALL, N. C.
C. T. CLOSS, Nebraska.
EUGENE F. HILL, Md.
JOHN L. CHADWICK, N. Y.
E. C. JOHNSON, Md.
A. N. HIRST, Pa.
VINCENT AUDINO MANERO, Porto Rico.
J. MATTHEWS, Cuba.
J. C. NORMEIL, Kansas.
NORMAN F. HILL, Md.
W. H. LEE, Md.
A. S. MATTHIAS, Md.
C. F. NALLY, D. C.
JOE ORNDORF, Md.
B. C. SPRINGFIELD, Tenn.
JOHN F. LEE, Md.
JOSE E. LANAS, Peru.
W. F. RUDOLPH, Mo.

———————◄•►———————

HONORARY MEMBERS.

Hon. WILLIAM GASTON North Carolina.
JOHN O'SULLIVAN, District Columbia.
Rev. PHILIP A. SACCHI, Georgetown College, District Columbia.
WILLIAM LAGGETT, New York.
U. C. YOUNG, Maryland.
JOHN SULLIVAN, District Columbia.

THEODORE JENKINS, Maryland.
JAMES HOBAN, District Columbia.
Z. COLLINS LEE, Maryland.
Rev. OLIVER JENKINS, Maryland.
Rev. P. CORRY, Maryland.
DONALD McLEOD, District Columbia.
JOHN E. DEVLIN, New York.

HONORARY MEMBERS—Continued.

Hon. JOHN M. S. CAUSIN, Maryland.

Hon. J. LEEDS KEER, Maryland.

WILLIAM A. STOKES, Pennsylvania.

Col. W. J. BLAKISTON, Maryland.

Hon. R. J. WALKER, ex-Secretary of the Treasury, Mississippi.

Hon. H. G. S. KEY, Maryland.

J. M. GILLIS, U. S. N., District Columbia.

Hon. WILLIAM COST JOHNSON, Md.

Hon. J. P. KENNEDY, Maryland.

O. A. BROWNSON, LL. D., Massachusetts.

JOHN ADDISON, California.

GEORGE W. PARKE CUSTIS, Virginia.

JOSEPH H. CLARKE, Maryland.

WILLIAM G. READ, LL. D., Maryland.

W. W. SEATON, ex-Mayor Washington.

JULES DERILLE, Gaudaloupe.

WILLIAM McDERMOTT, Dist. Columbia.

HENRY MAY, Baltimore.

Most Rev. JOHN HUGHES, Archbishop of New York.

Rev. JOHN McCAFFREY, D. D.

Lieut. MAURY, U. S. N., Dist. Columbia.

Prof. GRAFTON TYLER, M. D., Dist. Col.

Prof. W. A. AIKEN, M. D., LL. D., Maryland.

Gen. DUFF GREEN, District Columbia.

Col. CHARLES A. MAY, U. S. A.

Prof. J. F. MAY, M. D., District Columbia.

Hon. MORRIS LONGSTRETH, Penn.

JOHN F. ENNIS, District Columbia.

S. HUMES PORTER, District Columbia.

PERRY E. BROCCHUS, Alabama.

RICHARD CRAWFORD, Dist. Columbia.

Dr. HENRY A. FORD, Maryland.

D. JAMES MORGAN, District Columbia.

Prof. JOSHUA RILEY, M. D., Dist. Col.

PETER C. HOWLE, District Columbia.

Dr. EUSEBIUS JONES, New York.

ALPHONSE BARBOT, U. S. N., D. C.

ROBERT OULD, District Columbia.

RICHARD LAY, District Columbia.

Rev. THOMAS B. FOLEY, Dist. Columbia.

Hon. E. L. LOWE, LL. D., Governor of Maryland.

ZACHARY TAYLOR, ex-President U. S.

MILLARD FILLMORE, ex-President U. S.

Hon. RUFUS KING, Alabama.

Rev. Mr. FINOTT, Boston.

Hon. W. W. PAYNE, Virginia.

Prof. NOBLE YOUNG, M. D., Dist. Col.

Prof. C. H. LIEBERMAN, M. D., Dist. Col.

Prof. F. HOWARD, M. D., District Columbia.

Prof. J. ELLIOT, M. D., District Columbia.

Dr. J. M. AUSTIN, District Columbia.

Prof. J. W. H. LOVEJOY, M. D., D. C.

Prof. S. W. EVERETT, M. D., Dist. Col.

Rev. B. A. MAGUIRE, President of Georgetown College.

Rev. D. LYNCH, Georgetown College.

Dr. W. T. C. Du HAMEL, District Columbia

EDWARD S. McNERHANY, S. J., Georgetown College.

Hon. R. McCLELLAND, Secretary of Int.

Hon. JAS. CAMPBELL, Postmaster General.

Hon. B. J. SEMMES, M. D., Prince George's County, Maryland.

Rev. Prof. J. CURLEY, S. J., Georgetown College.

Hon. THOMAS H. BENTON, Mo.

Rev. J. P. DONELAN, Prince George's Co., Maryland.

Honorable E. C. CABELL, Florida.

Rev. J. R. PLUNKET, Martinsburg, Va.

Hon. WILLIAM PRESTON, Kentucky.

Rev. T. J. O'TOOLE, D. D., Washington, D. C.

Hon. ROBERT J. BRENT, Baltimore, Md.

Rev. GEORGE C. CARROLL, S. J., Ohio.

Hon. WILLIAM D. MERRICK, Maryland.

ALEXANDER GARESCHE, Missouri.

J. H. MADIGAN.

Rev. A. McMULLIN.

Rev. JOHN FORCE.

Dr. J. M. SNYDER.

J. McSHERRY.

THEODORE J. TALBOT.

Hon. CHARLES GAYARRE, Louisiana.

R. J. BOWIE.

Hon. FRANKLIN PIERCE, ex-Pres. U. S.

YATES WALSH.

HONORARY MEMBERS—Continued.

Rev. J. M. ARDIA.

C. E. GRENAUX, Sr., Louisiana.

Rev. CHARLES KING.

Rev. FRANCIS BOYLE.

Judge P. A. ROST, Louisiana.

CHARLES W. RUSSELL.

Dr. J. G. GOULLSTON.

Rev. LEONARD NOTA.

Rev. BENEDICT SESTINI.

G. MORRIS, California.

W. H. HOYT.

Prof. G. C. SCHAEFFER, M. D.

Rev. EDWARD H. WELCH, S. J.

Rev. A. VAN DEN HEUVEL, S. J.

Rev. PATRICK DUDDY, S. J.

Rev. EDMUND YOUNG, S. J.

Rev. JOHN WOOLTZ, S. J.

MICHAEL DRACO DIMITRY, Louisiana.

CHAS. M. GRIMM, Maryland.

Rev. E. A. KNIGHT.

Dr. ANTICELLE, District Columbia.

Right Rev. BISHOP O'CONOR, Penn.

Rev. JOS. O'CALLAGHAN, President of Loyola College, Baltimore.

Rev. ROBERT FULTON.

C. C. MAGRUDER, Maryland.

JESUS ESCOBAR, Mexico.

C. W. HOFFMAN, Maryland.

DANIEL FORD, S. J., Georgetown College.

GEORGE J. STRONG, S. J., Georgetown College.

JOS. H. KING, S. J., Georgetown College.

T. B. KEYES, Maryland.

JOHN L. SUMNER, S. J., Maryland.

HENRY MAJOR, Pennsylvania.

C. CARVALLO, Pennsylvania.

SIGNIOR ASTABURUAGA, Chili.

SIGNIOR MATHIAS ROMERO. Mexico.

WILLIAM SUMNER, S. J., Maryland.

Rev. ALOYSIUS JANELICK, Austria.

Prof. VARSI, Italy.

Rev. JOS. O'HAGAN, S. J., Georgetown College.

Rev. J. B. MULLALY, S. J., Georgetown College.

Dr. F. W. TONER, District Columbia.

W. B. NICODEMUS, Esq., Virginia.

Hon. S. T. RANDAL, Pennsylvania.

Hon. D. W. VOORHIES, Ia.

Rev. STEPHEN KELLY, S. J., D. C.

Hon. O. W. BROWNNING, Illinois.

Gen. THOS. EWING, Kansas.

EDWARD W. BELT, Esq., Maryland.

Gen. ROBERT E. LEE, Virginia.

Dr. THOMAS MILLER, District Columbia.

Prof. NOBLE S. HOFFER, Dist. Columbia.

Prof. CHAS. BUNTING, Maryland.

JOHN F. CALLAN, Esq., Dist. Columbia.

Gen. ROBERT WILLIAMS, Dist. Columbia.

Maj. JOHN F. LEE, Maryland.

Prof. JULIUS SOPER, District Columbia.

Gen. HORACE PORTER, U. S. A.

WILLIAM M. HILL, Maryland.

Gen. BRADLEY T. JOHNSON, Virginia.